OCT - - 2023

Dear Parent:

Psst . . . you're looking at the Super Secret Weapon of Reading. It's called comics.

STEP INTO READING® COMIC READERS are a perfect step in learning to read. They provide visual cues to the meaning of words and helpfully break out short pieces of dialogue into speech balloons.

Here are some terms commonly associated with comics:

PANEL: A section of a comic with a box drawn around it.
CAPTION: Narration that helps set the scene.
SPEECH BALLOON: A bubble containing dialogue.
GUTTER: The space between panels.

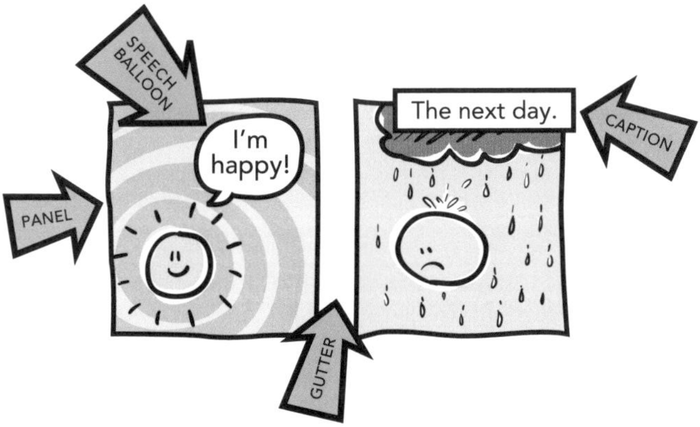
SPEECH BALLOON
I'm happy!
PANEL
The next day.
CAPTION
GUTTER

Tips for reading comics with your child:

- **Have your child read the speech balloons while you read the captions.**
- **Ask your child: What is a character feeling? How can you tell?**
- **Have your child draw a comic showing what happens after the book is finished.**

STEP INTO READING® COMIC READERS are designed to engage and to provide an empowering reading experience. They are also fun. The best-kept secret of comics is that they create lifelong readers. ***And that will make you the real hero of the story!***

Jennifer L. Holm and Matthew Holm
Co-creators of the Babymouse and Squish series

Published in the United States by Random House Children's Books, a division of Penguin Random House LLC, 1745 Broadway, New York, NY 10019, and in Canada by Penguin Random House Canada Limited, Toronto, in conjunction with Sesame Workshop.

Step into Reading, Random House, and the Random House colophon are registered trademarks of Penguin Random House LLC.

Visit us on the Web!
www.sesamestreet.org
rhcbooks.com

Educators and librarians, for a variety of teaching tools, visit us at RHTeachersLibrarians.com

ISBN 978-0-593-64456-0 (trade) — ISBN 978-0-593-64458-4 (ebook) —
ISBN 978-0-593-64457-7 (lib. bdg.)

Printed in the United States of America
10 9 8 7 6 5 4 3 2 1

Random House Children's Books supports the First Amendment and celebrates the right to read.

A COMIC READER

STEP INTO READING®

STEP 2

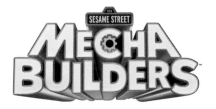

SESAME STREET MECHA BUILDERS

The Super-Duper Magnet!

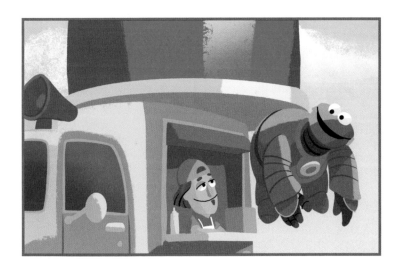

adapted by Lauren Clauss
based on the episode "Magnet Mayhem"
written by Andrew Moriarty
illustrated by Shane Clester

Random House New York

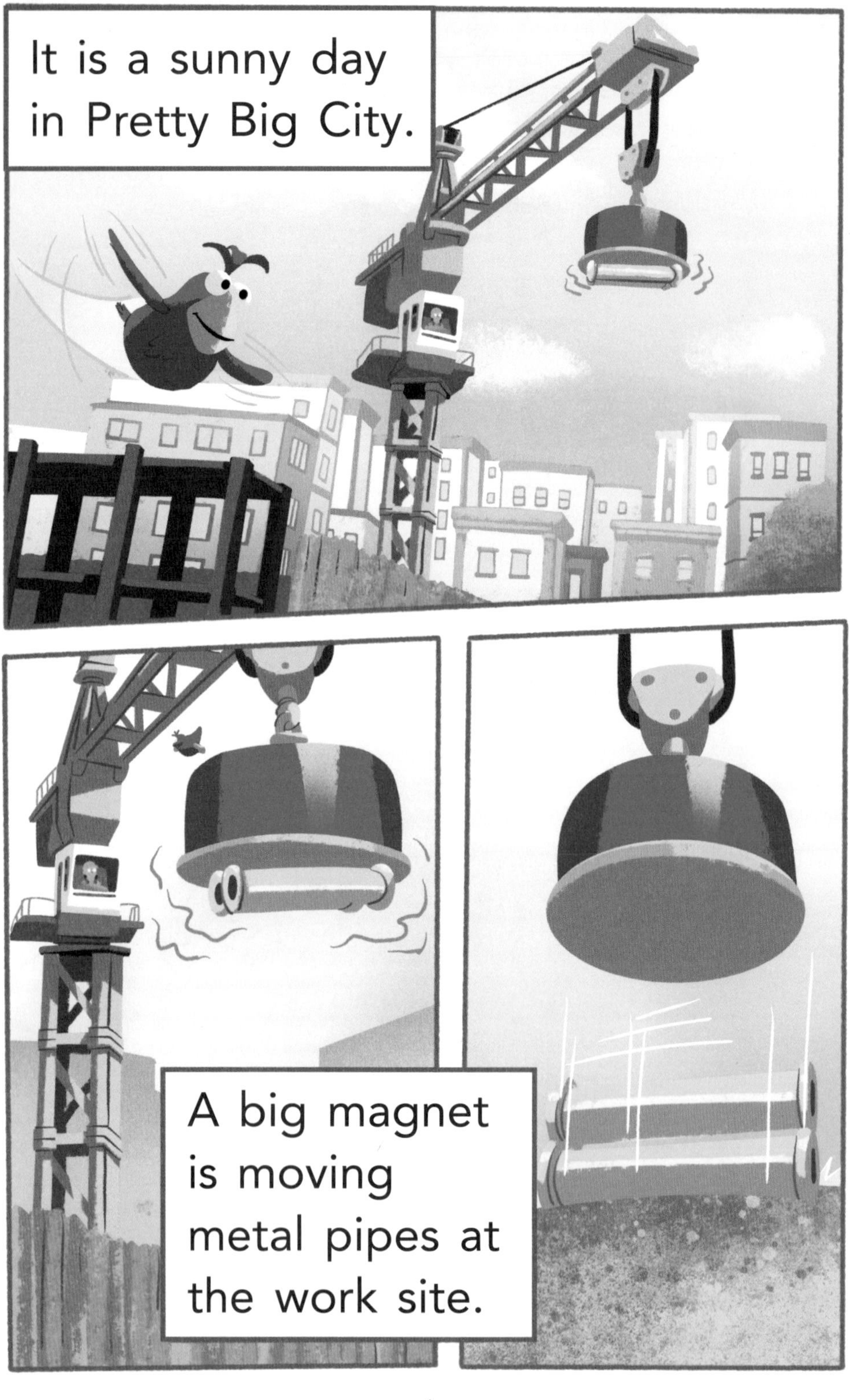
It is a sunny day in Pretty Big City.
A big magnet is moving metal pipes at the work site.

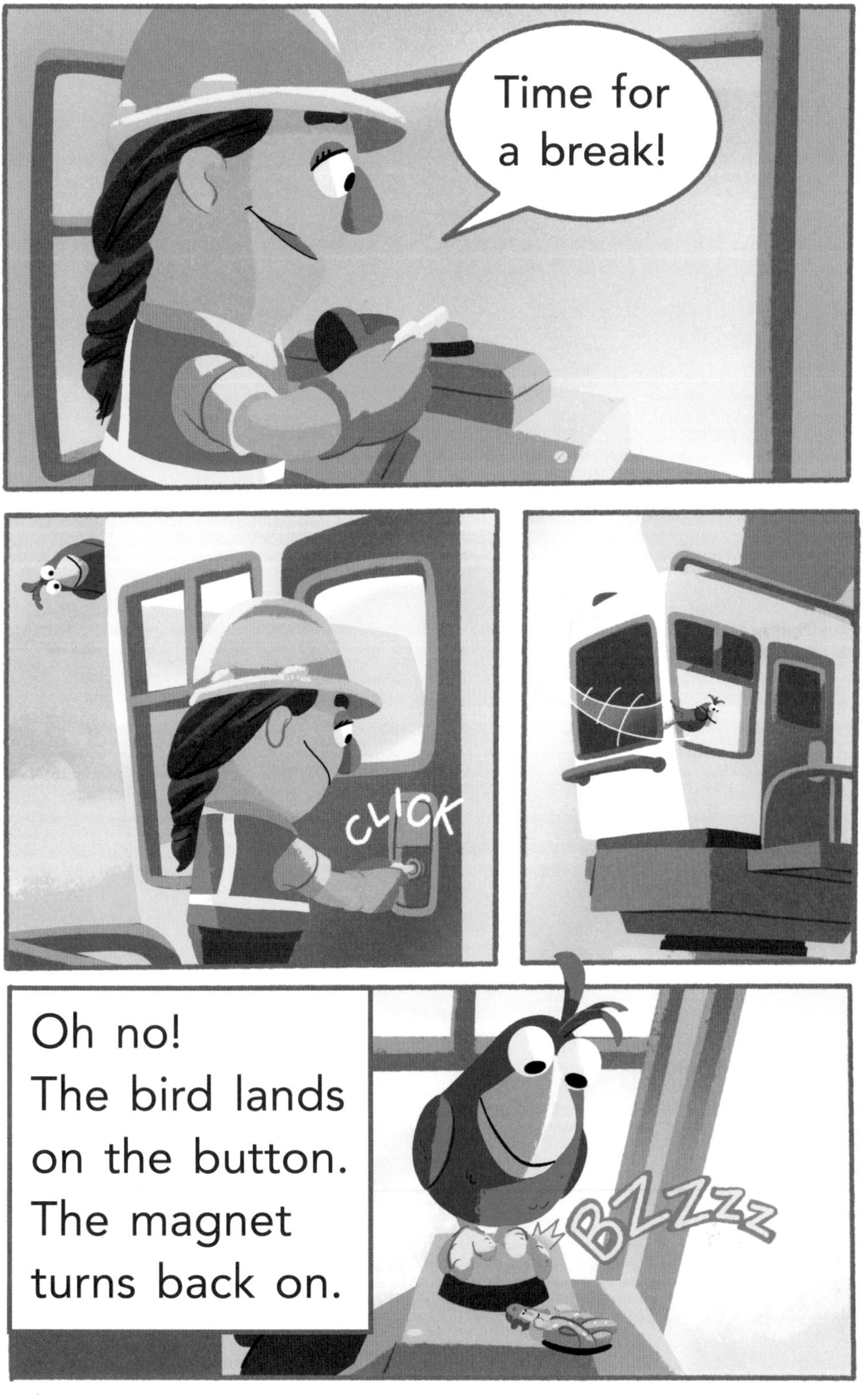
Time for a break!
CLICK
Oh no!
The bird lands on the button.
The magnet turns back on.
BZZzz

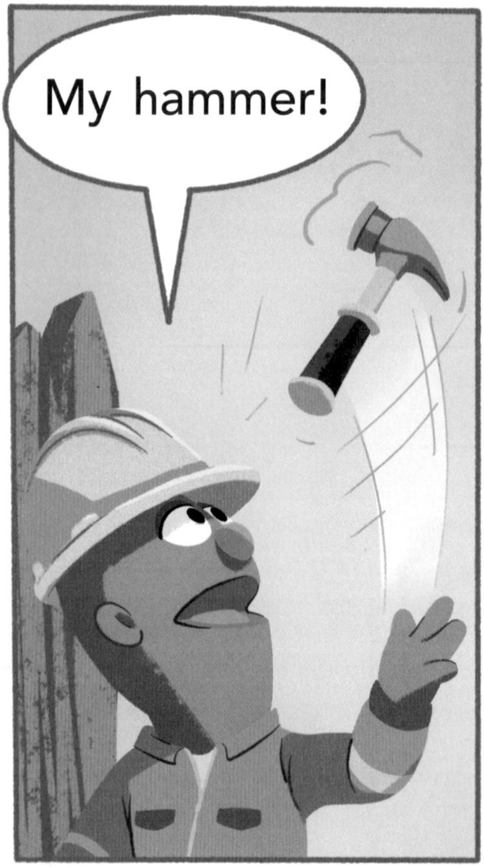
My hammer!

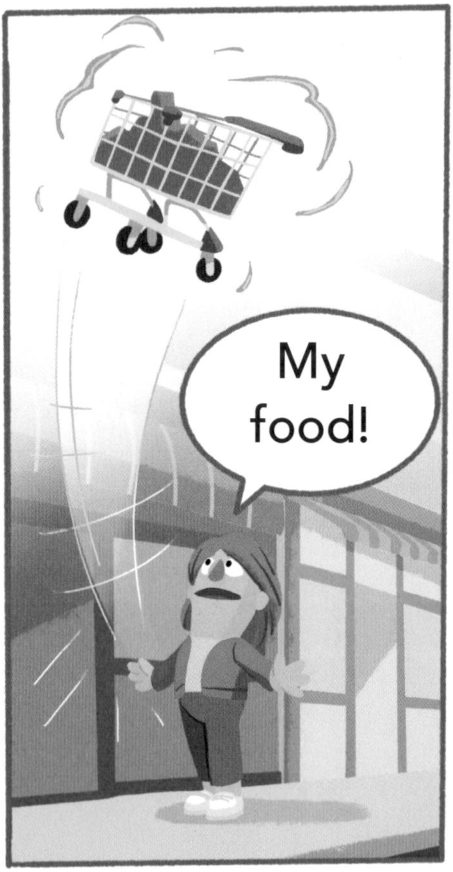
My food!

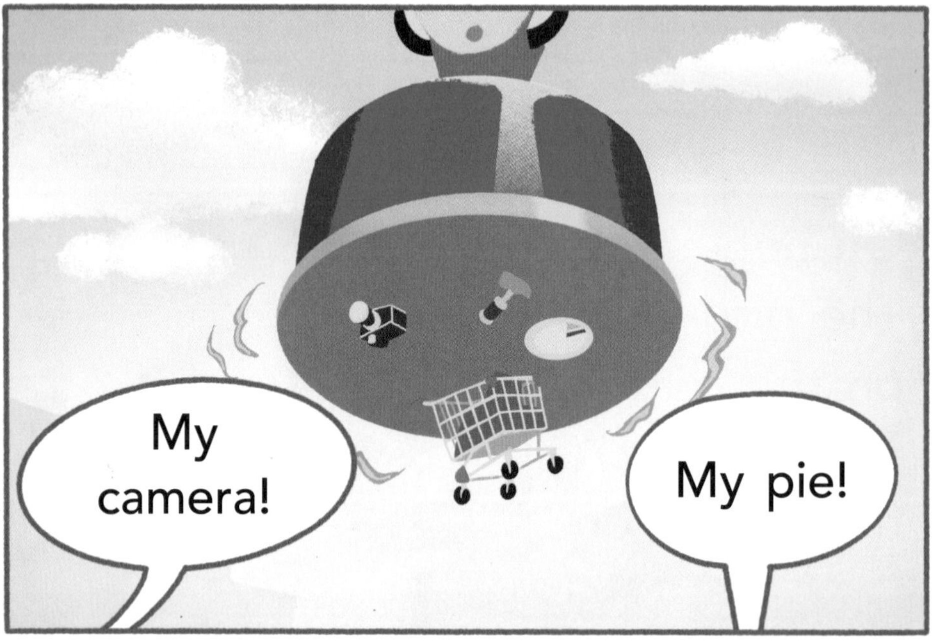
My camera!
My pie!

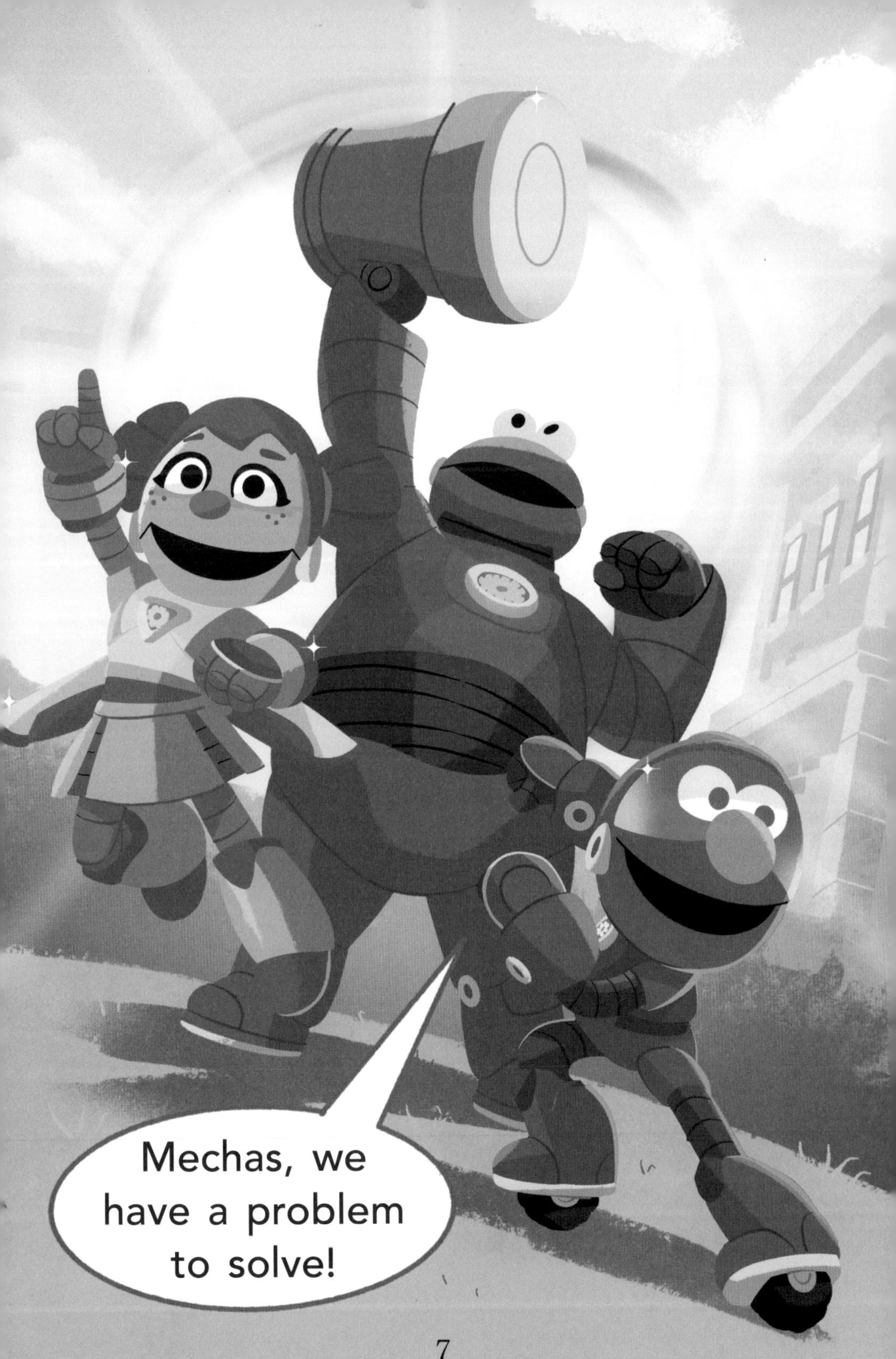
Mechas, we have a problem to solve!

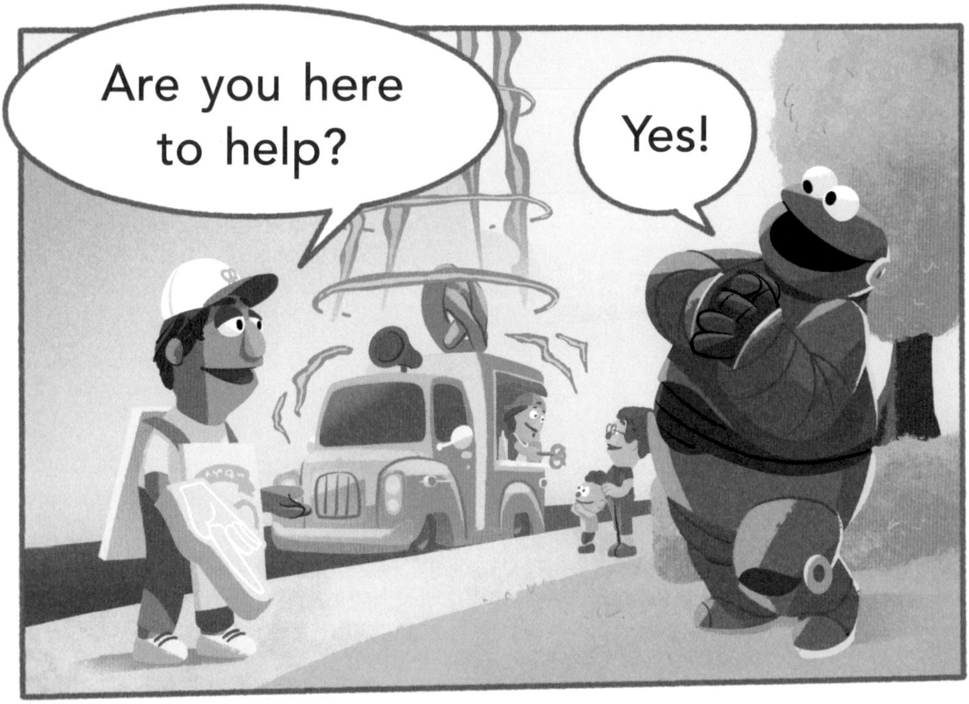
Are you here to help?
Yes!

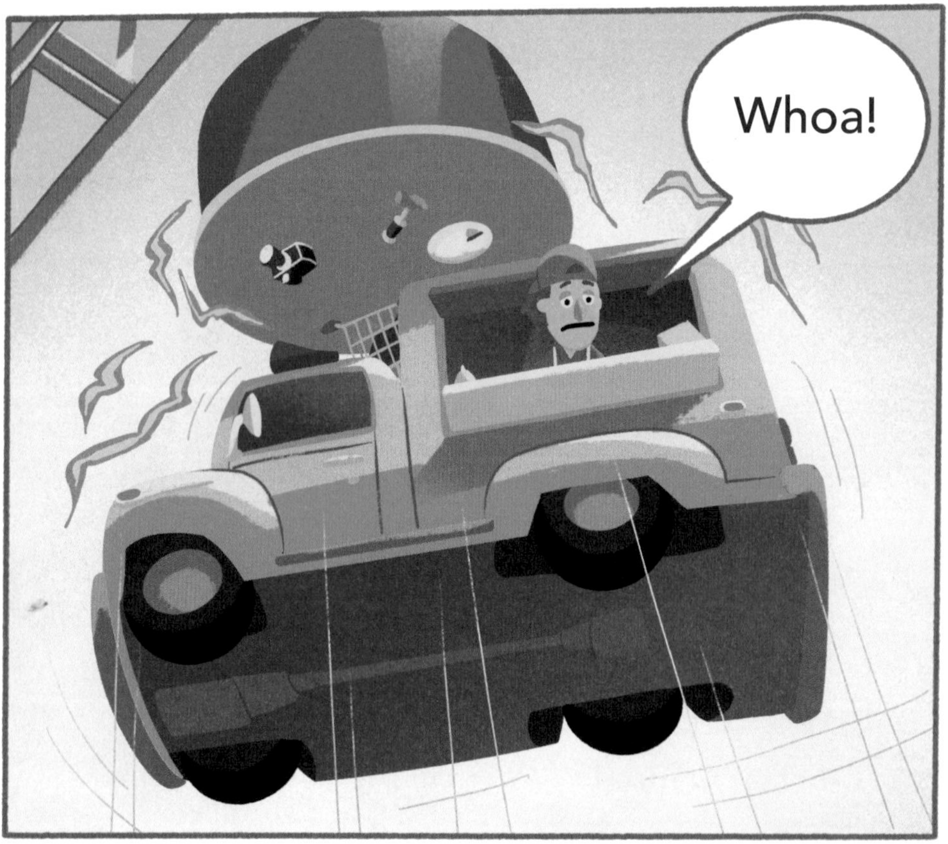
Whoa!

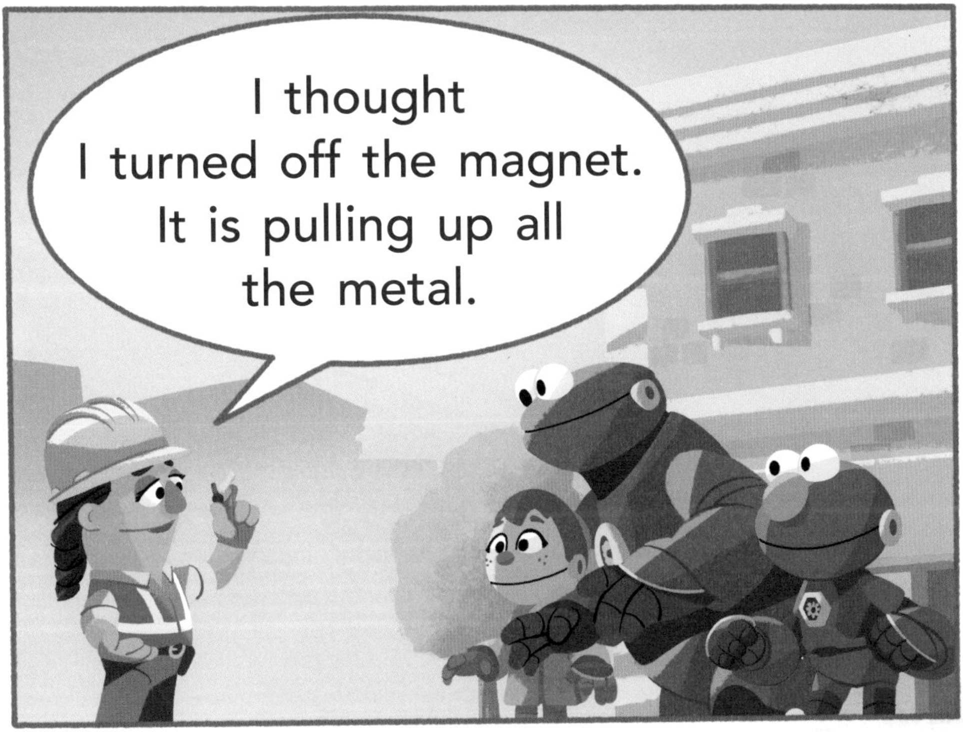
I thought I turned off the magnet. It is pulling up all the metal.

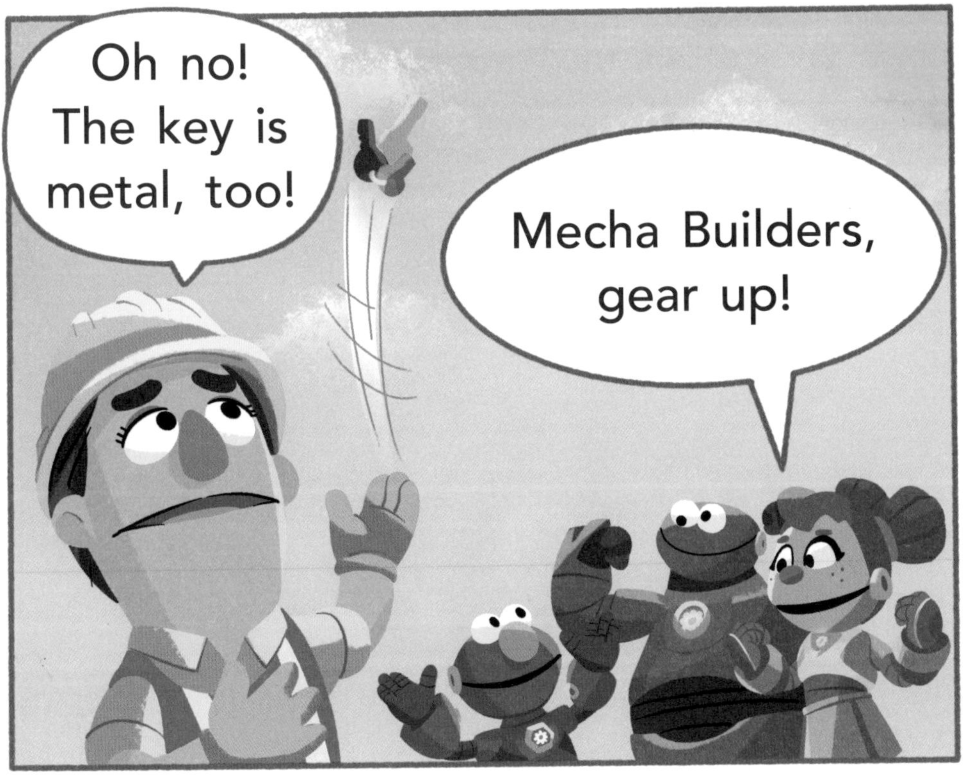
Oh no! The key is metal, too!
Mecha Builders, gear up!

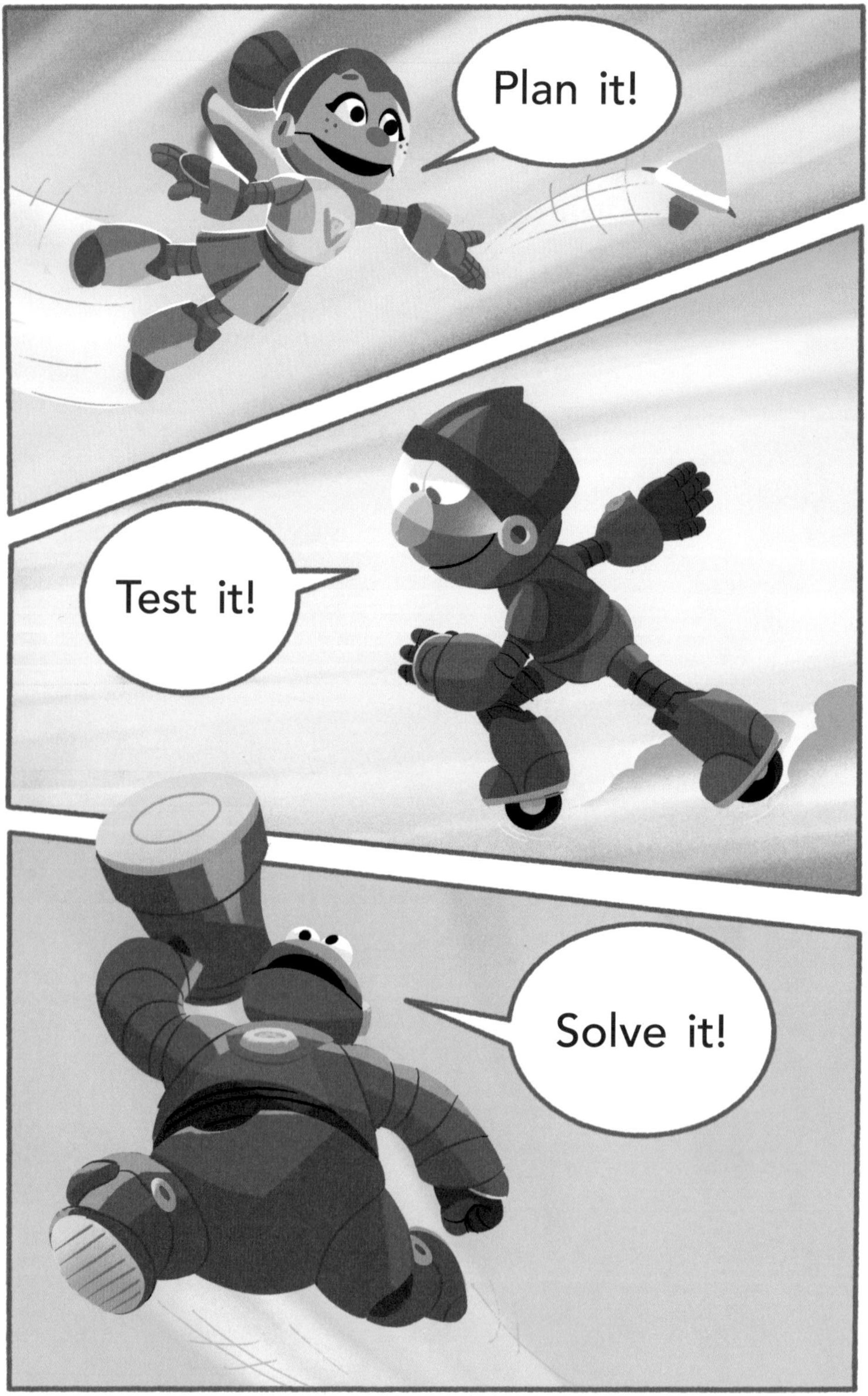
Plan it!
Test it!
Solve it!

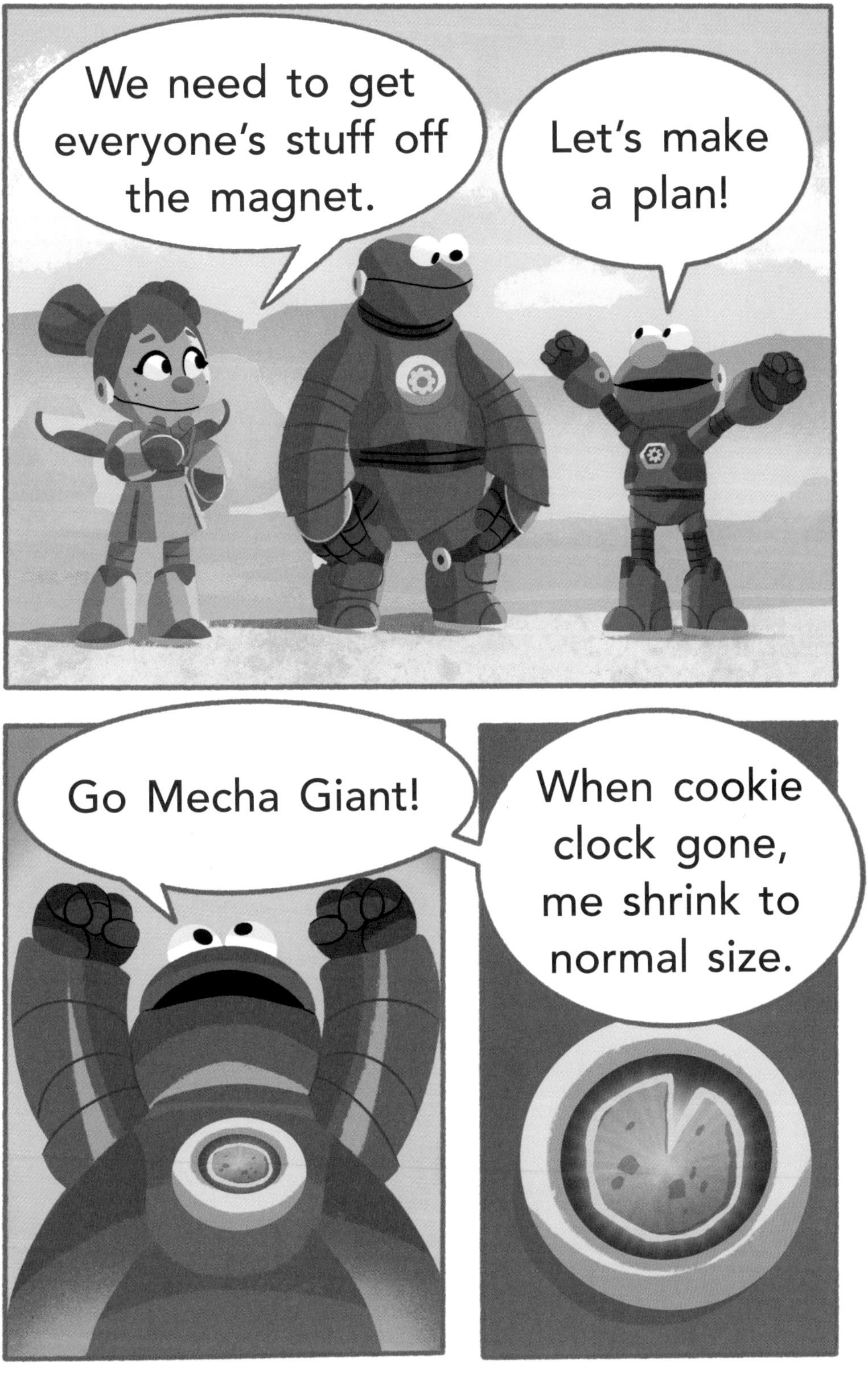
We need to get everyone's stuff off the magnet.
Let's make a plan!
Go Mecha Giant!
When cookie clock gone, me shrink to normal size.

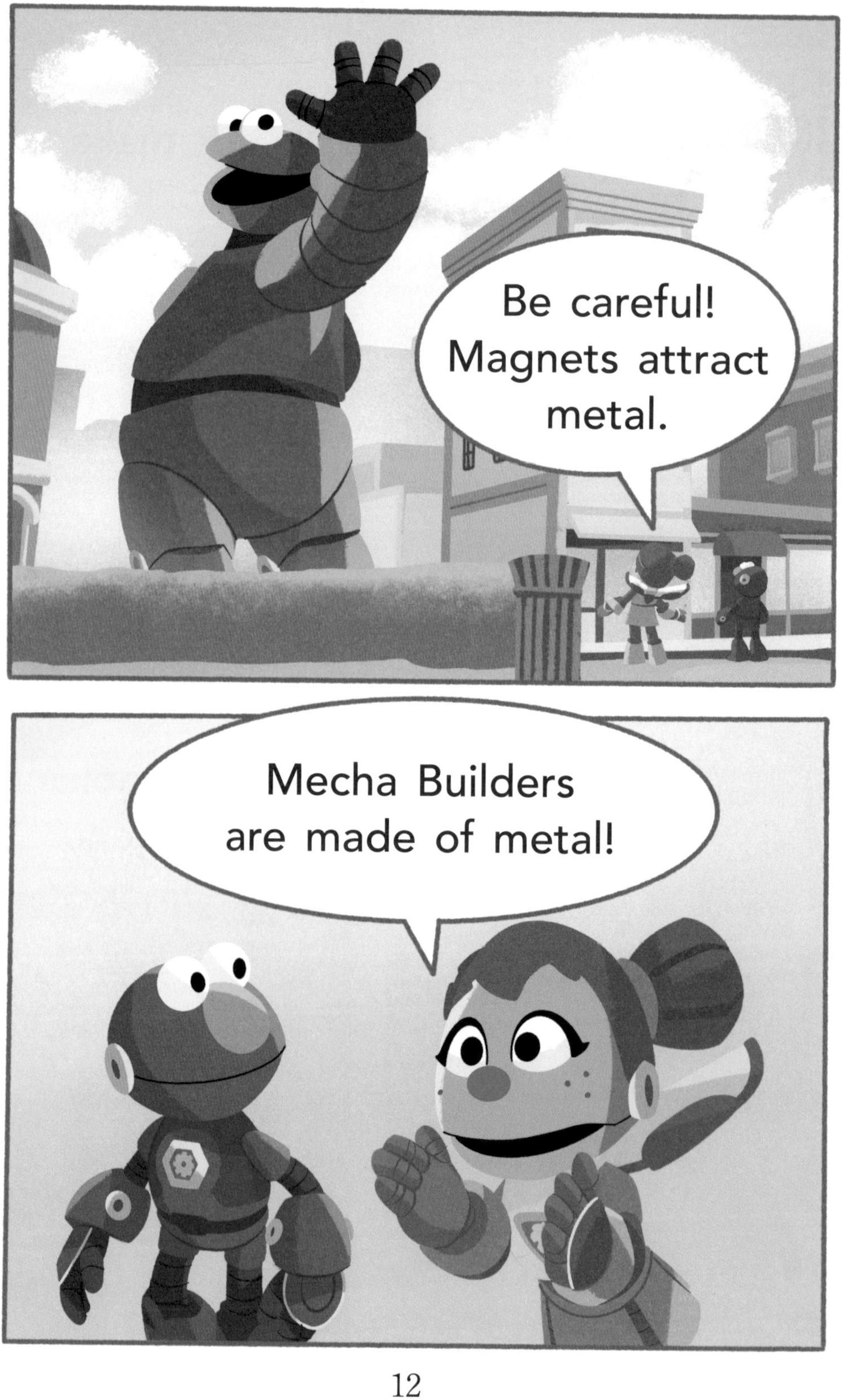
Be careful! Magnets attract metal.
Mecha Builders are made of metal!

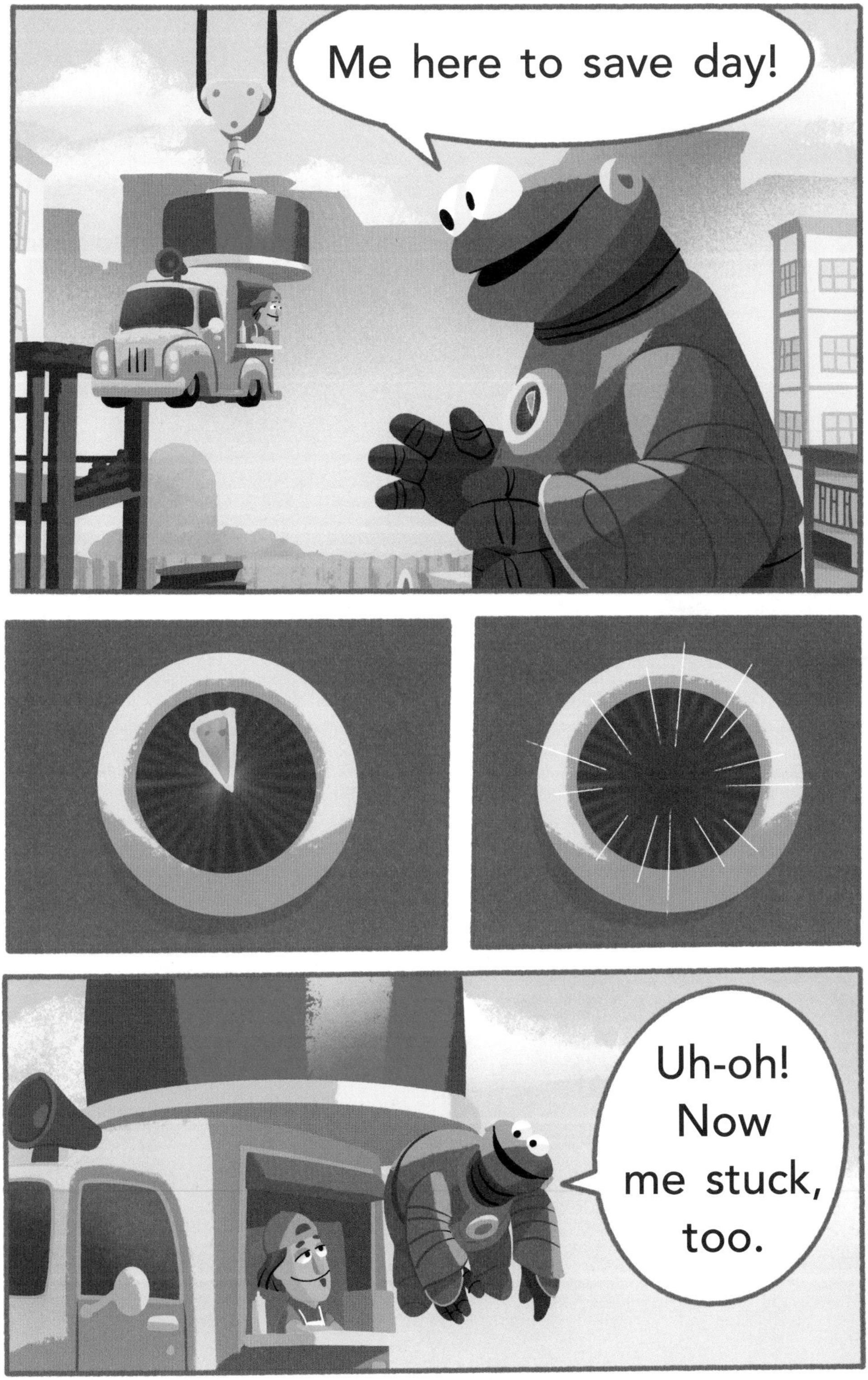
Me here to save day!
Uh-oh! Now me stuck, too.

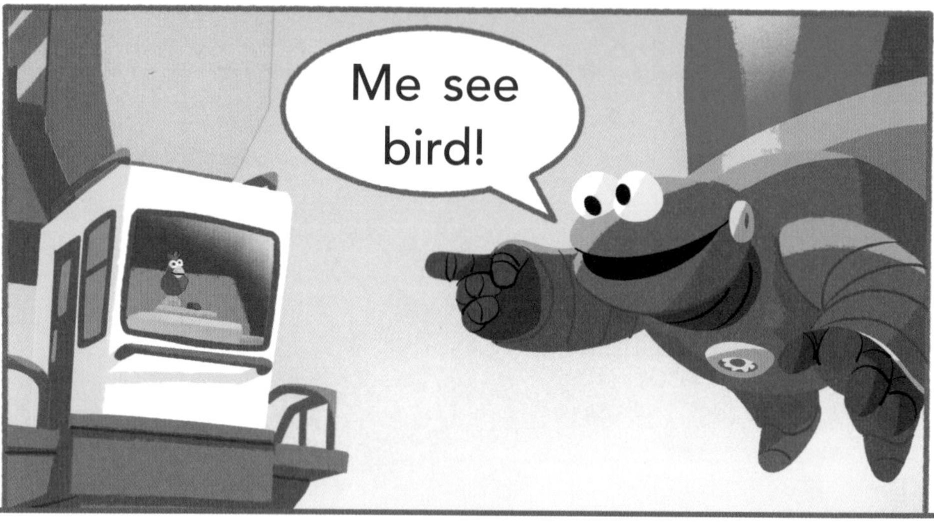
Me see bird!

Mecha Cookie also sees a big red button.

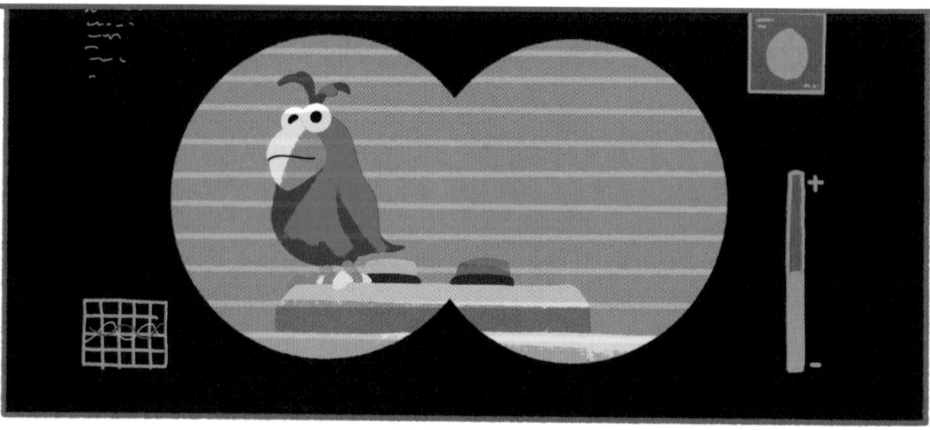

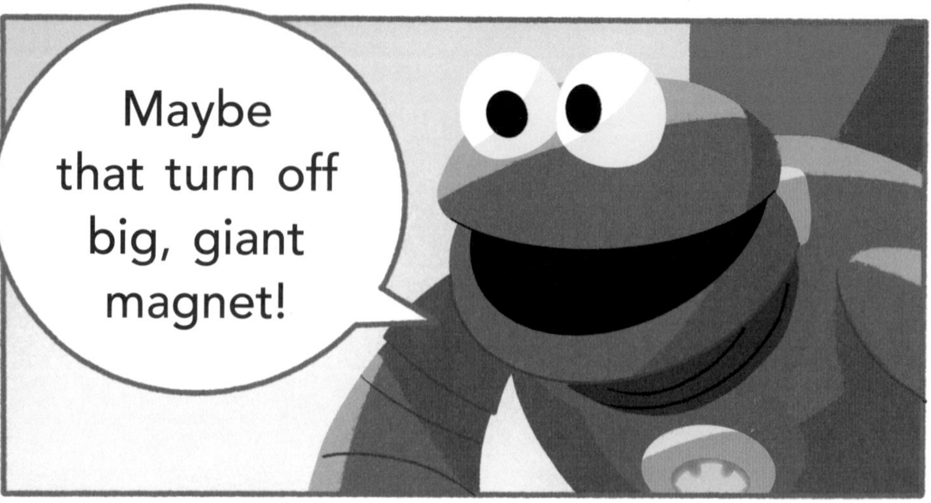
Maybe that turn off big, giant magnet!

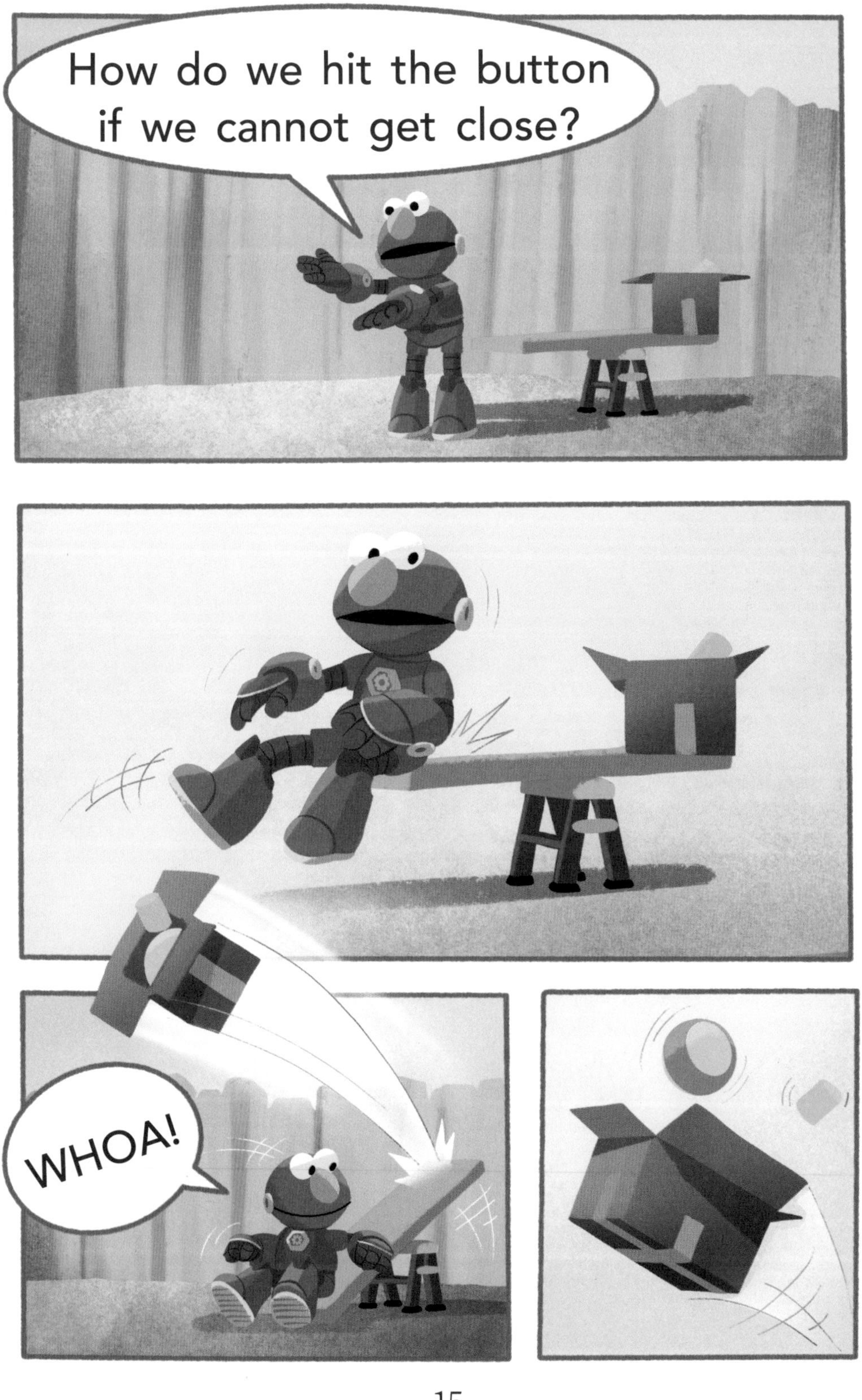
How do we hit the button if we cannot get close?
WHOA!

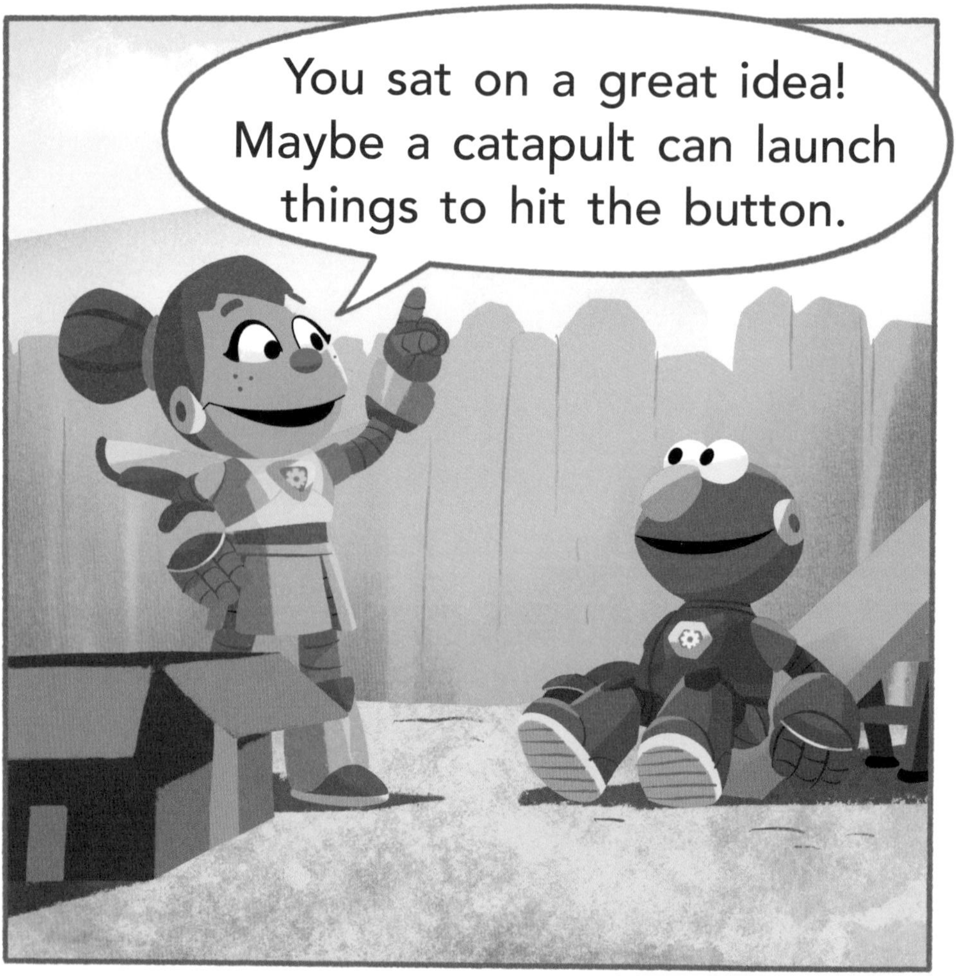
You sat on a great idea! Maybe a catapult can launch things to hit the button.

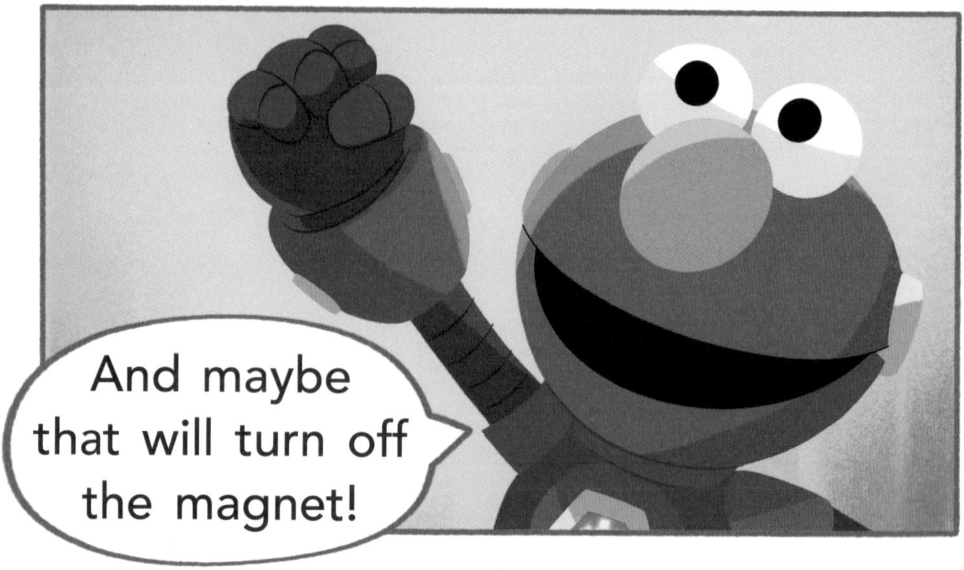
And maybe that will turn off the magnet!

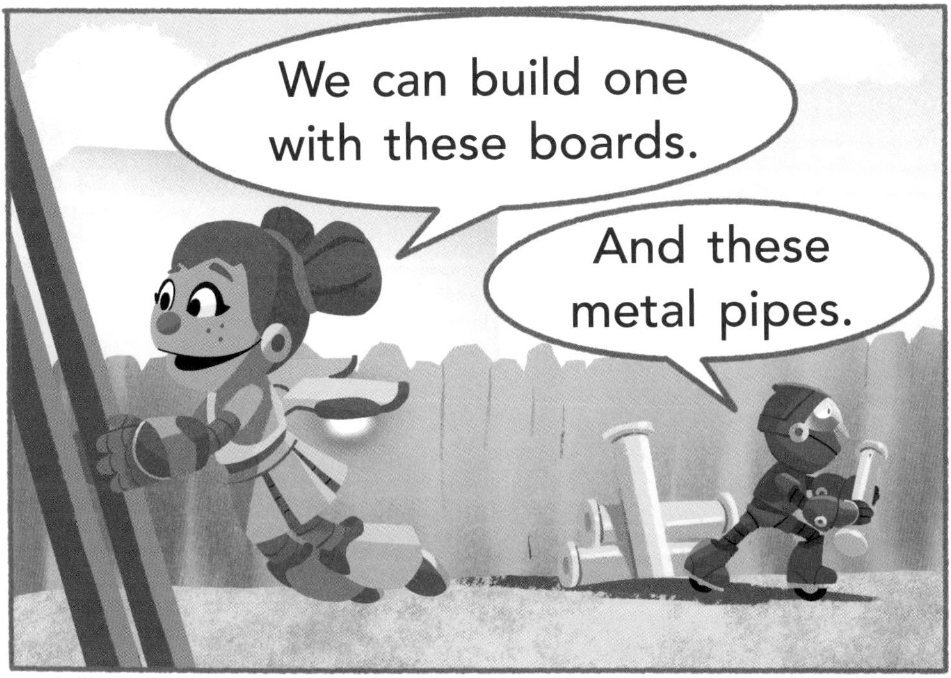
We can build one with these boards.
And these metal pipes.

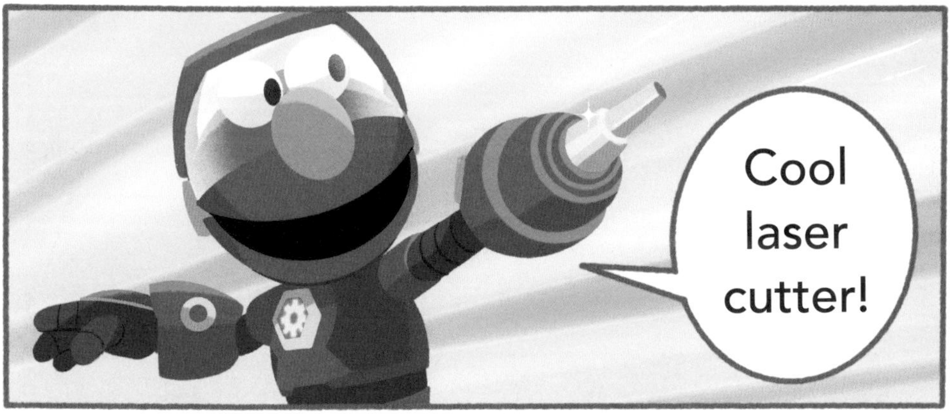
Cool laser cutter!

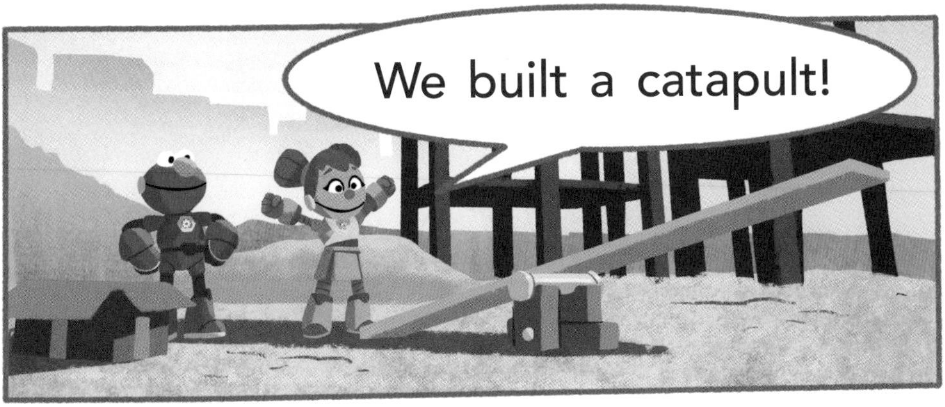
We built a catapult!

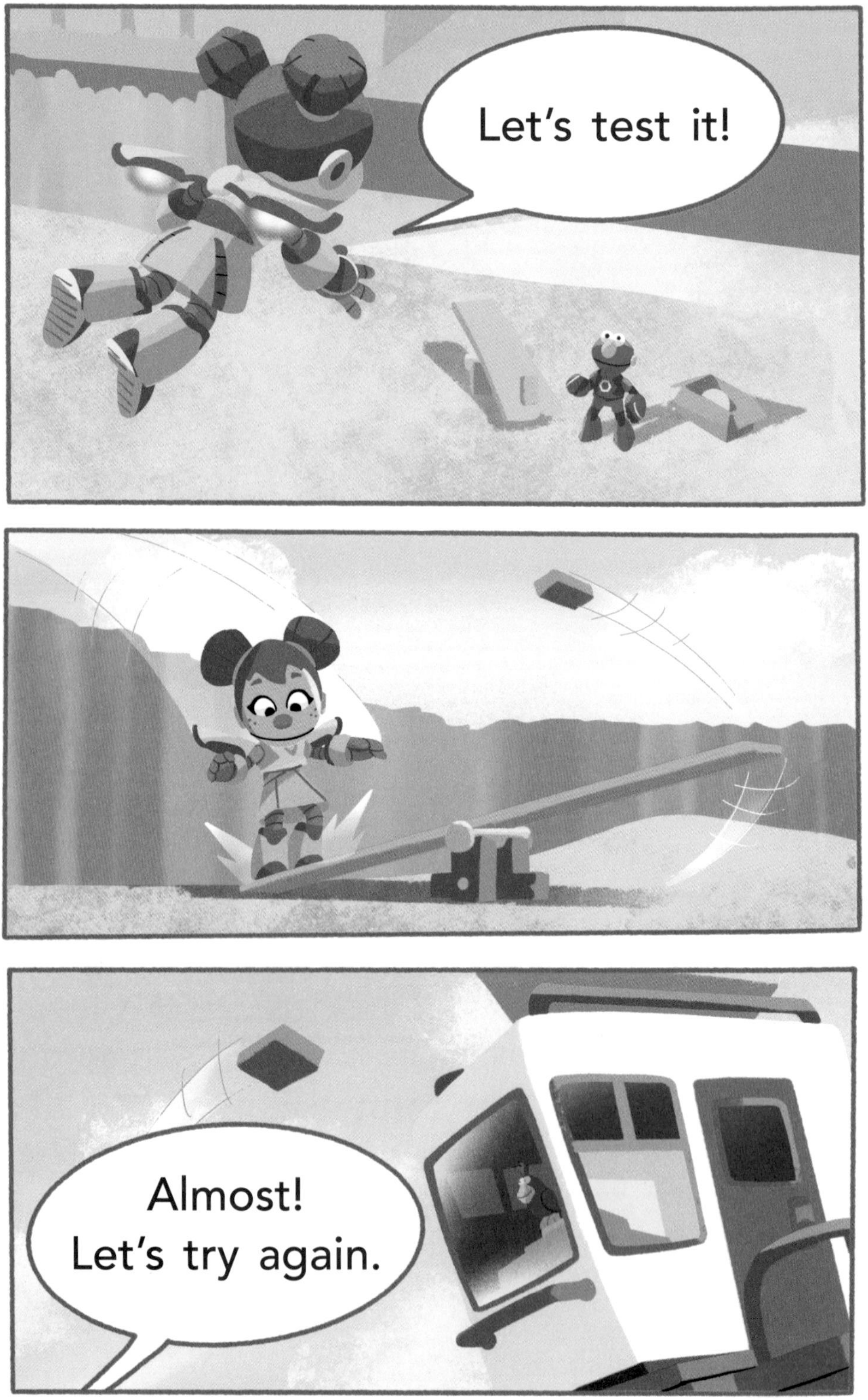
Let's test it!
Almost!
Let's try again.

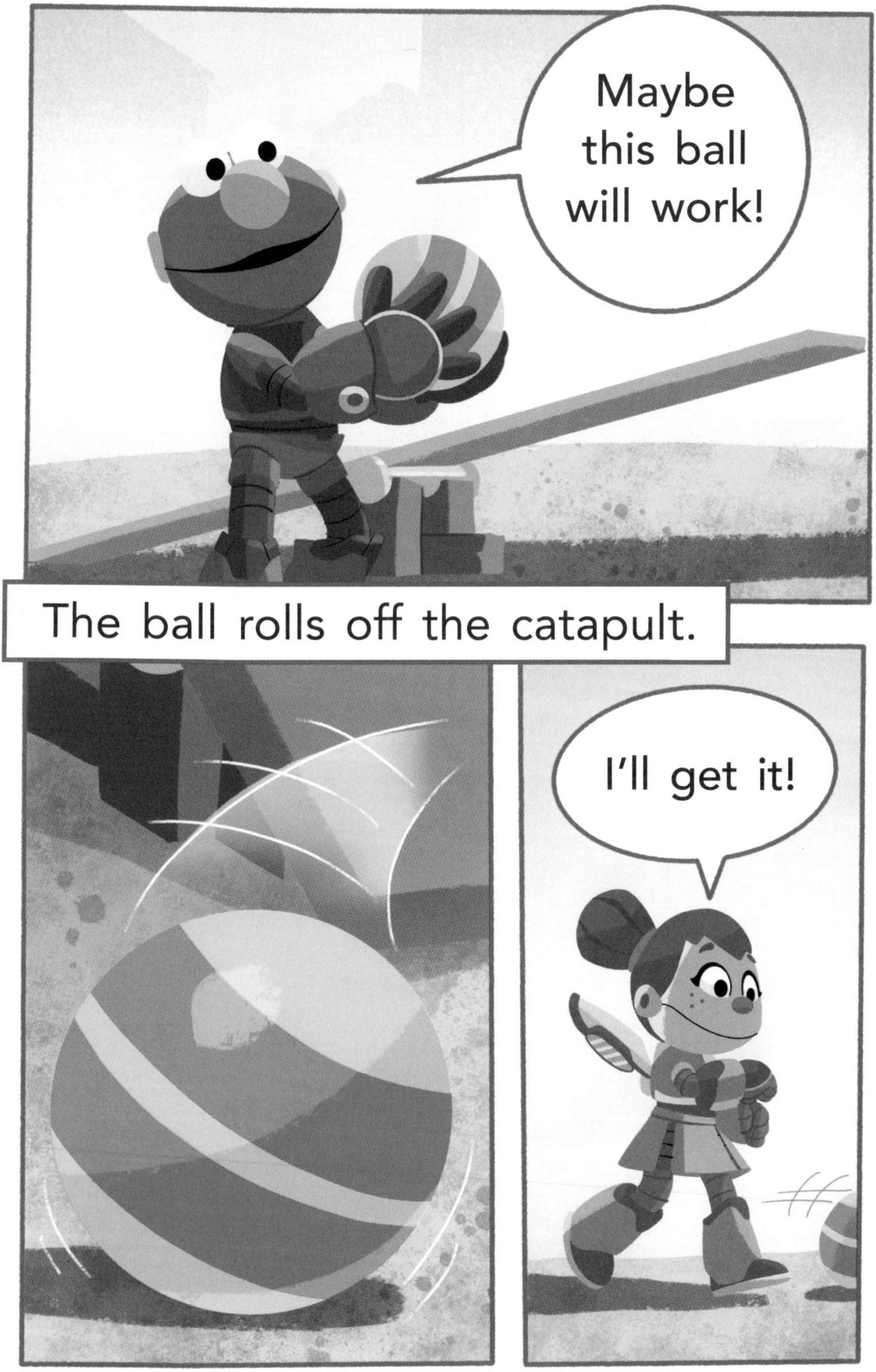
Maybe this ball will work!
The ball rolls off the catapult.
I'll get it!

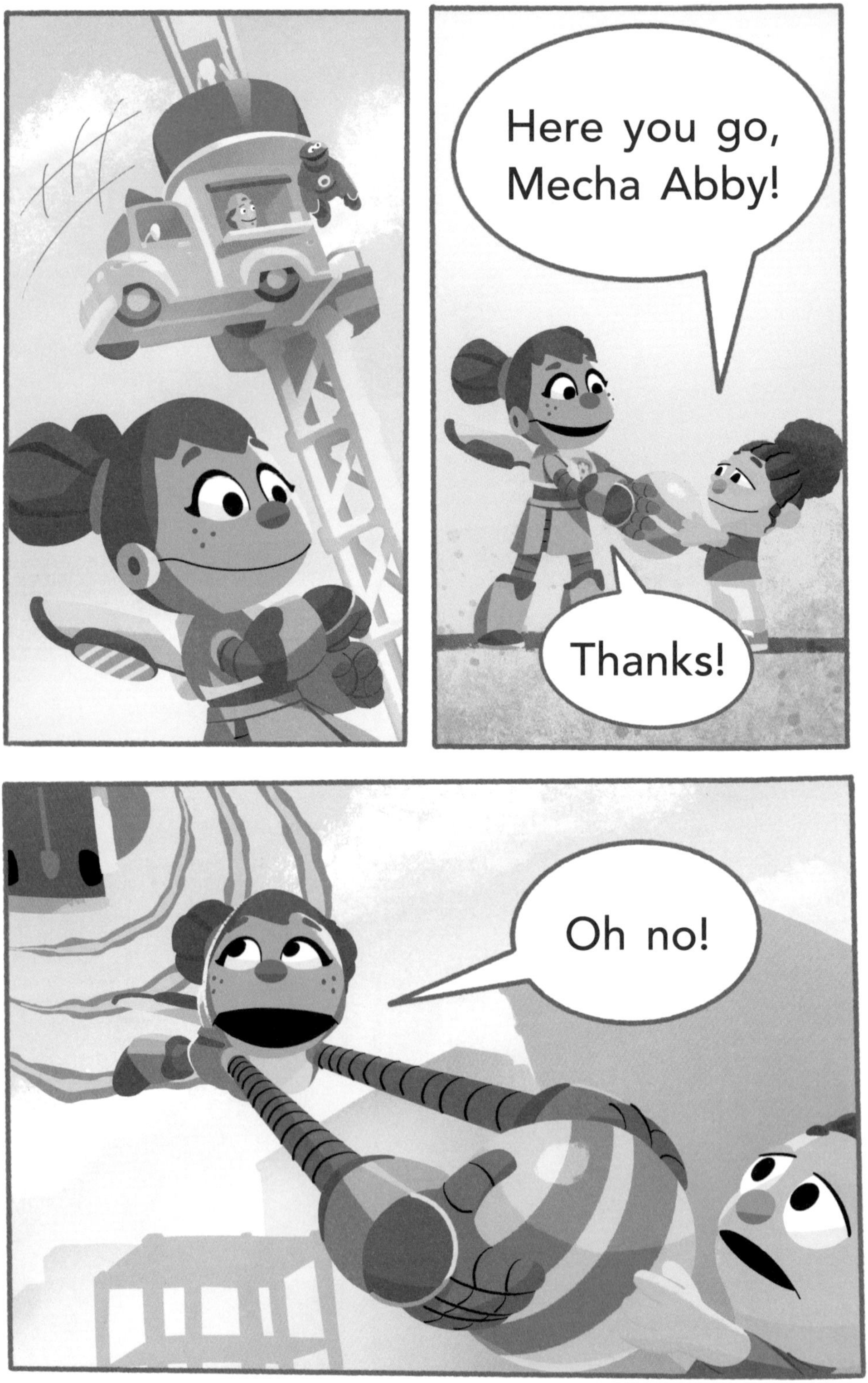
Here you go, Mecha Abby!
Thanks!
Oh no!

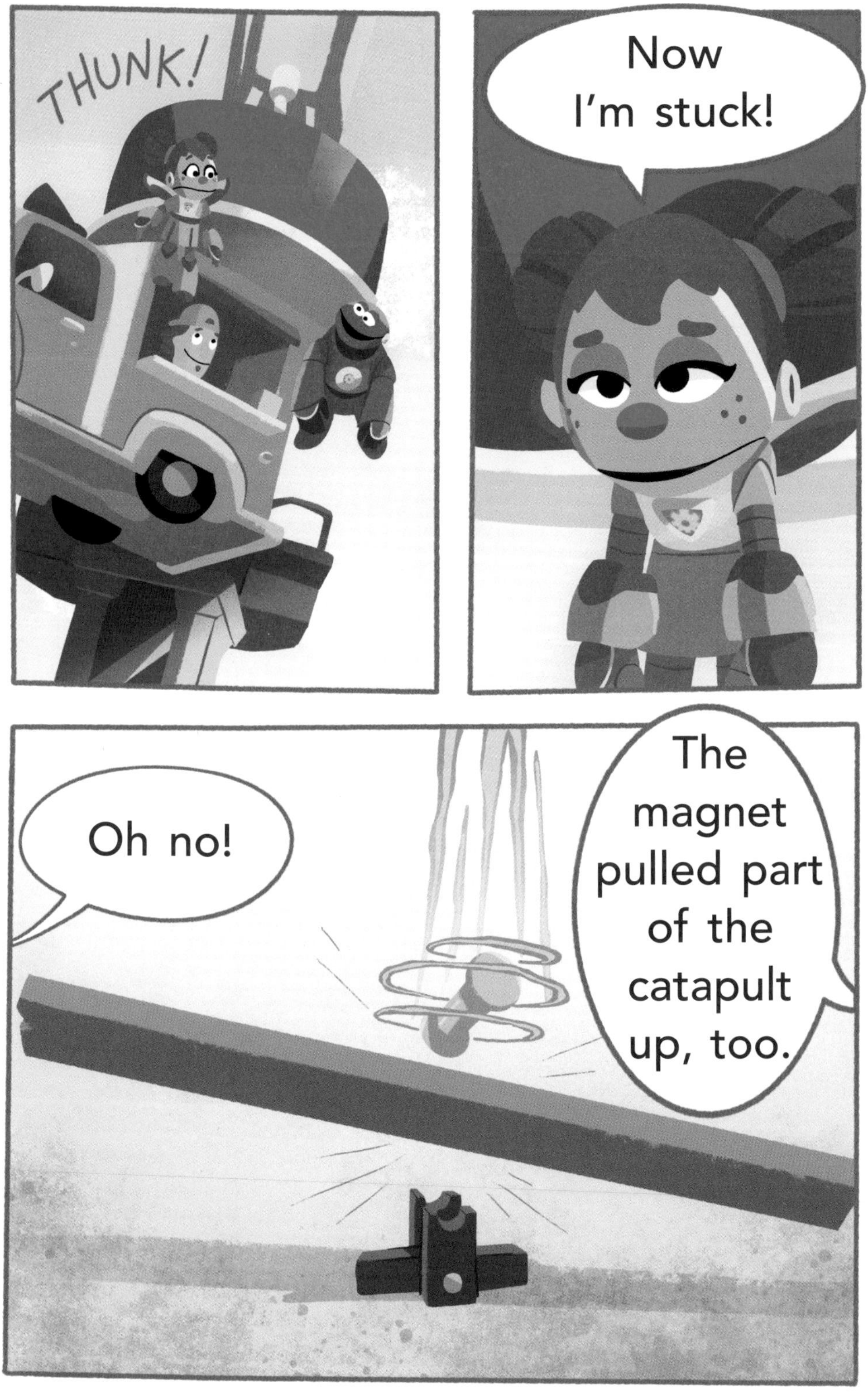
THUNK!
Now I'm stuck!
Oh no!
The magnet pulled part of the catapult up, too.

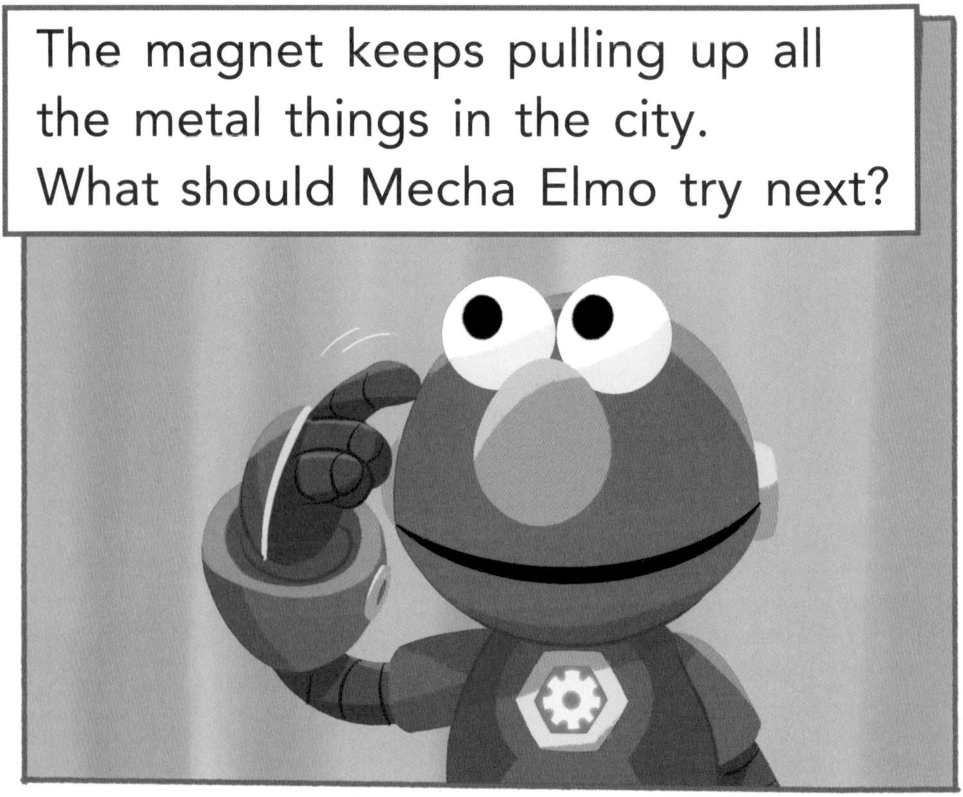
The magnet keeps pulling up all the metal things in the city. What should Mecha Elmo try next?

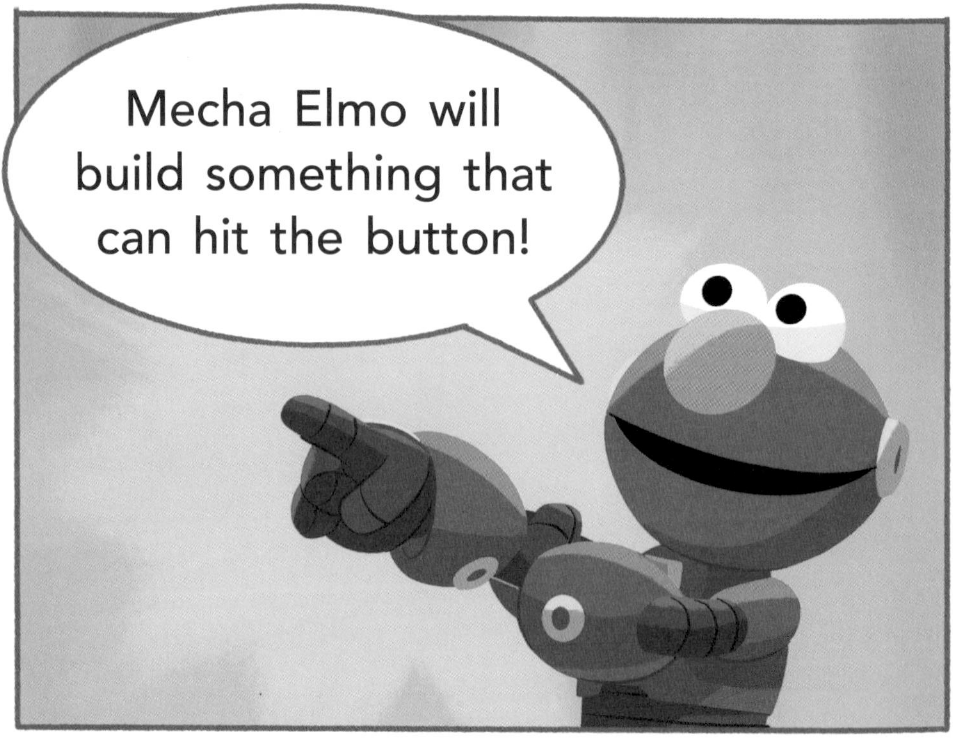
Mecha Elmo will build something that can hit the button!

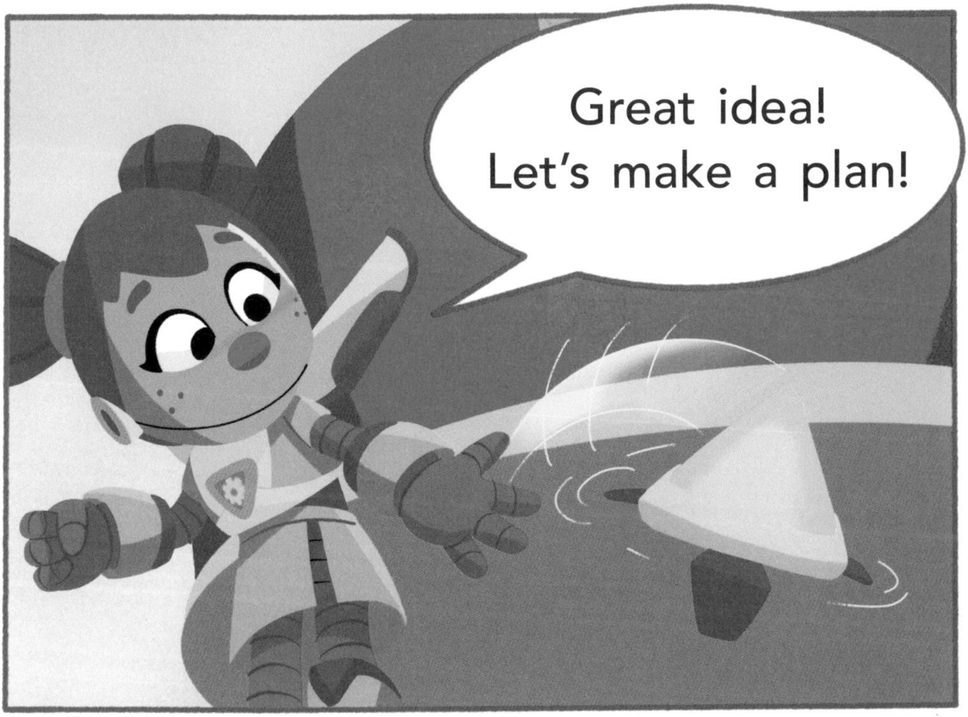
Great idea!
Let's make a plan!

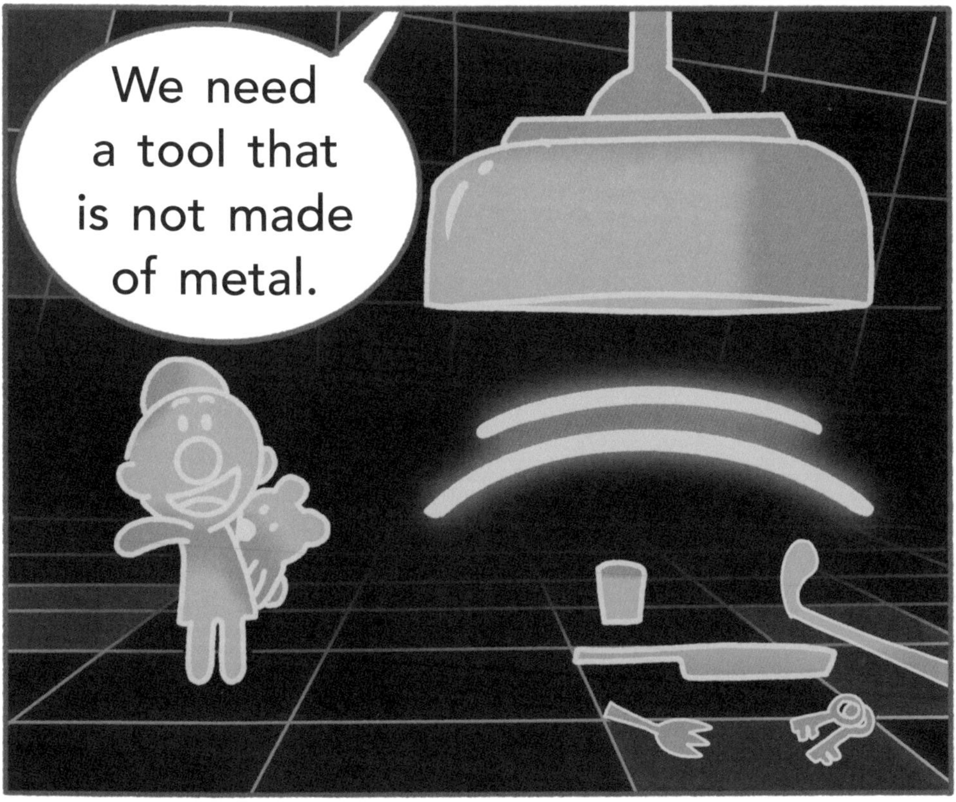
We need a tool that is not made of metal.

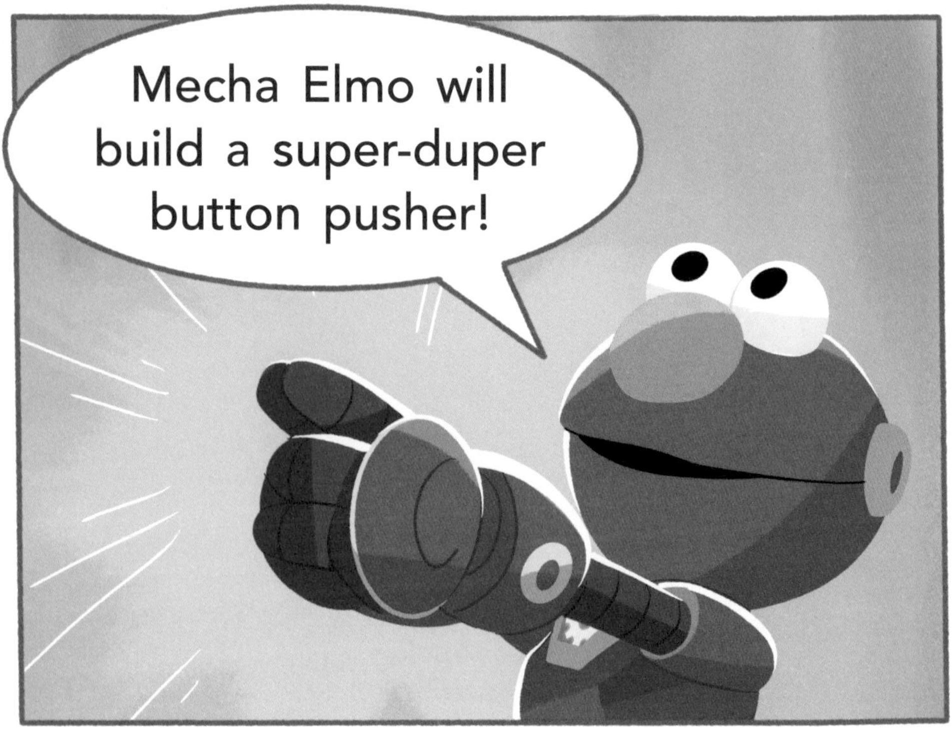
Mecha Elmo will build a super-duper button pusher!

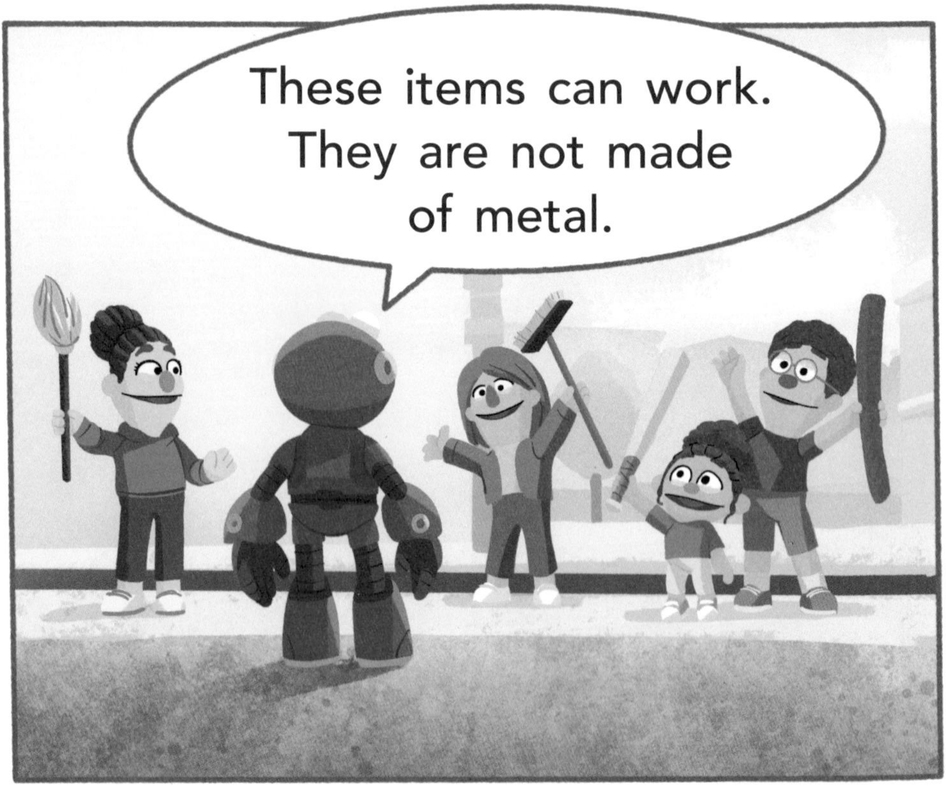
These items can work. They are not made of metal.

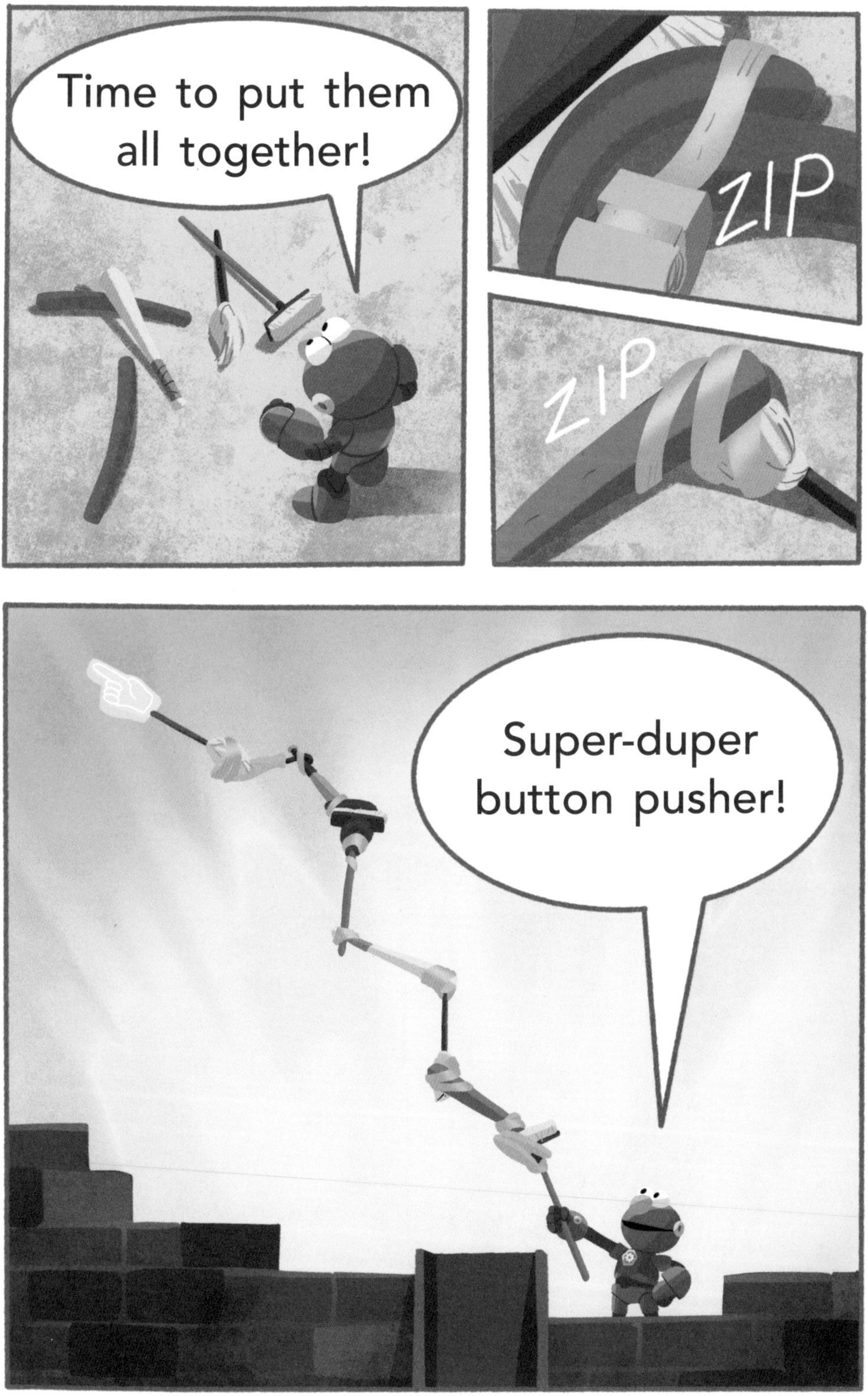
Time to put them all together!
ZIP
ZIP
Super-duper button pusher!

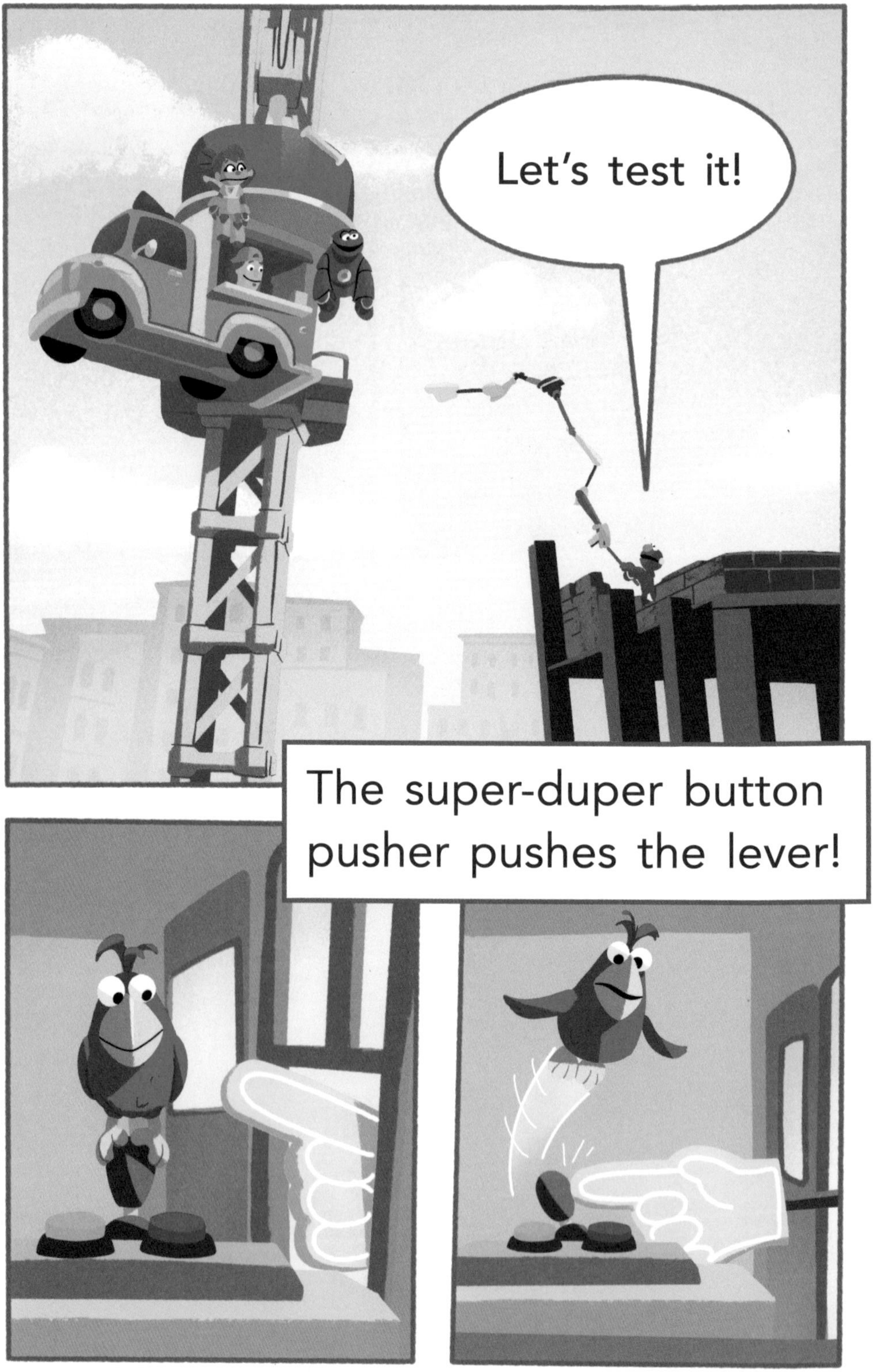
Let's test it!
The super-duper button pusher pushes the lever!

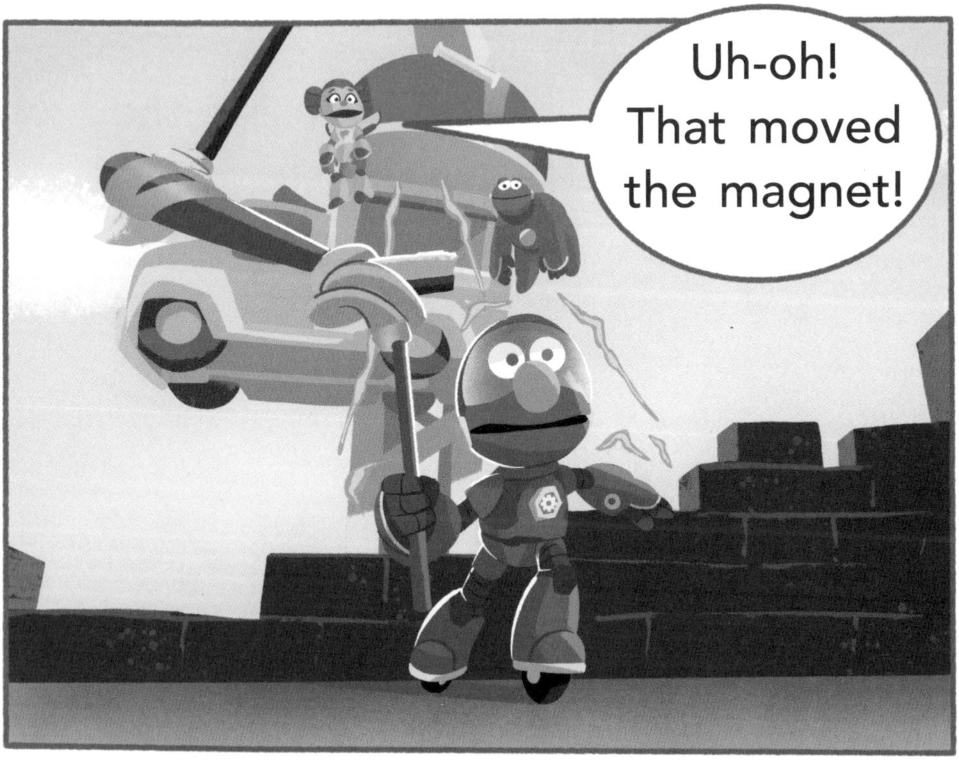
Uh-oh! That moved the magnet!

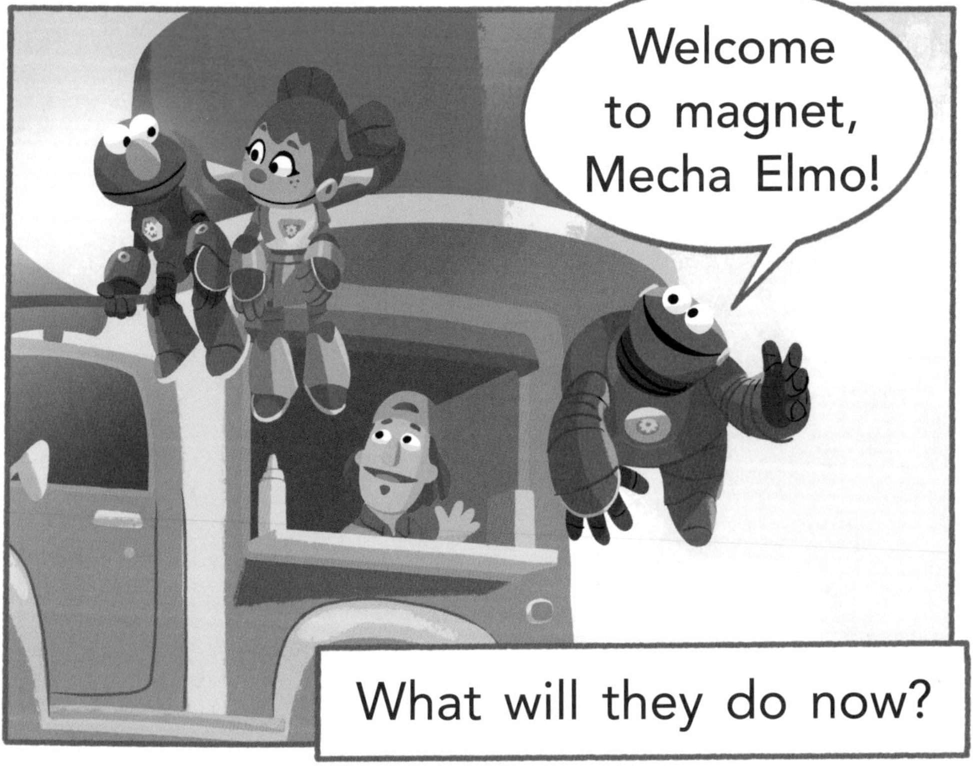
Welcome to magnet, Mecha Elmo!
What will they do now?

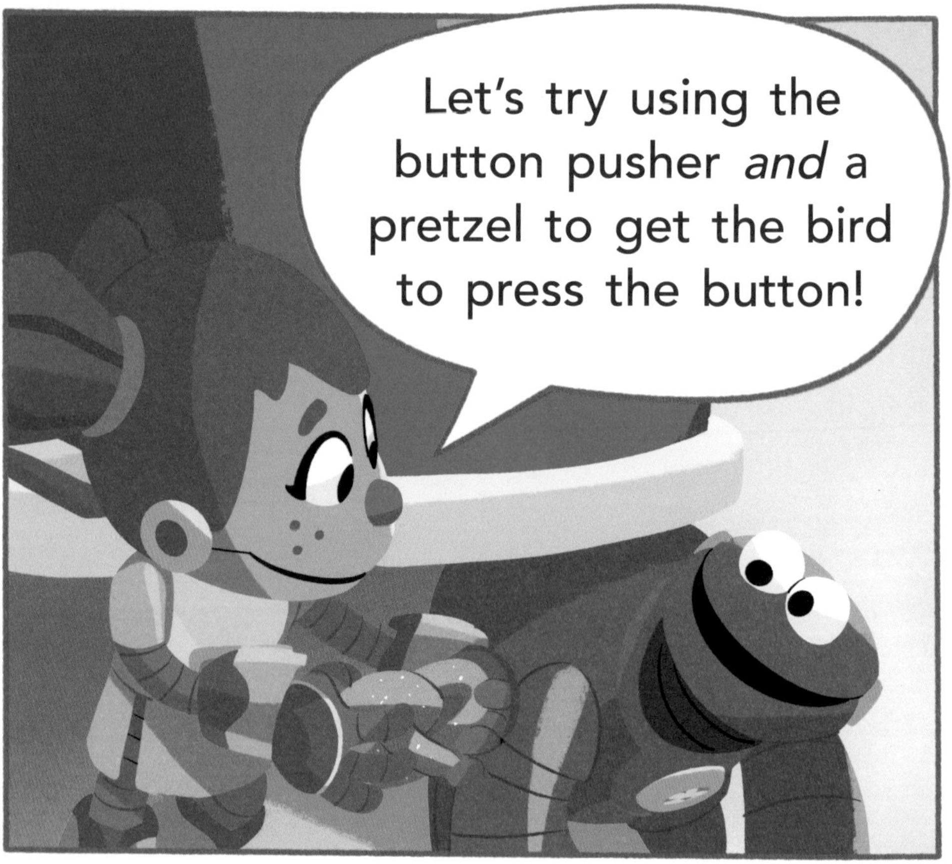
Let's try using the button pusher *and* a pretzel to get the bird to press the button!

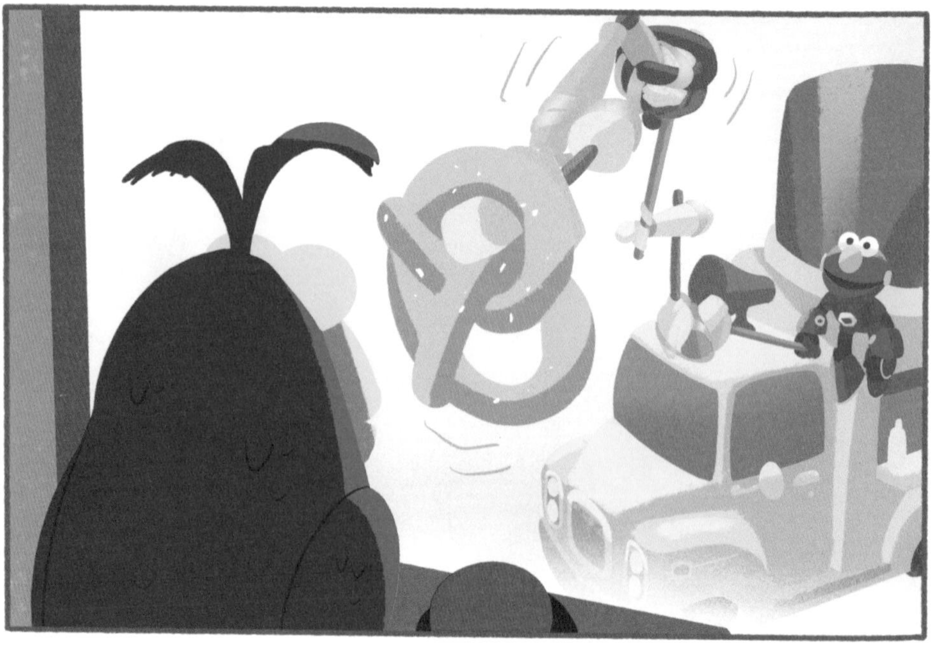

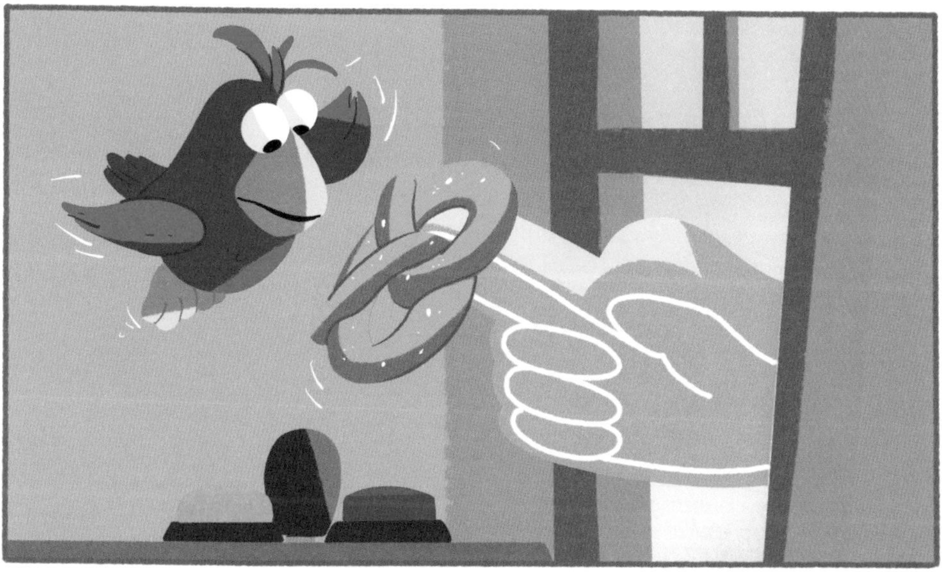

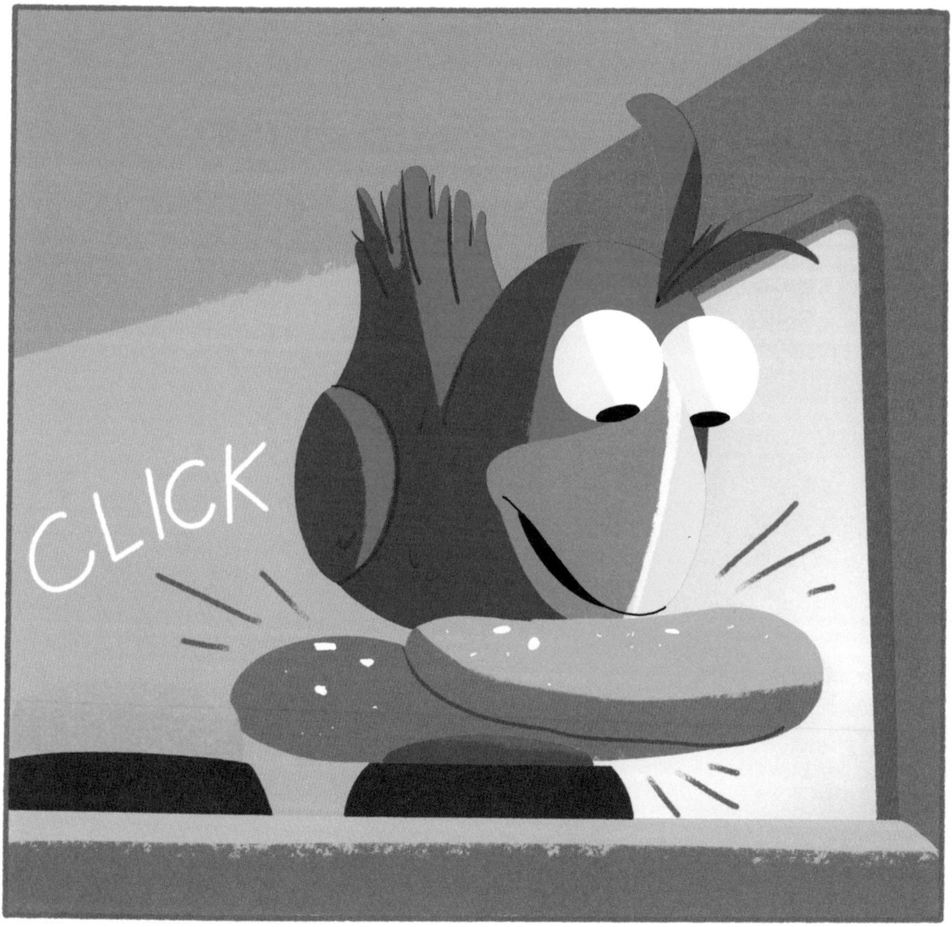
CLICK

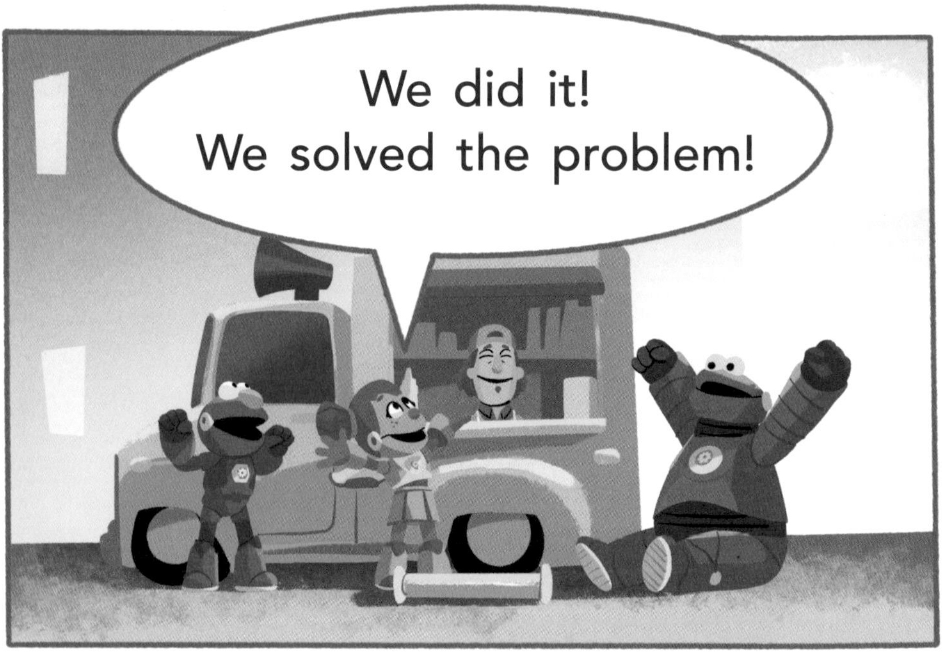
We did it!
We solved the problem!

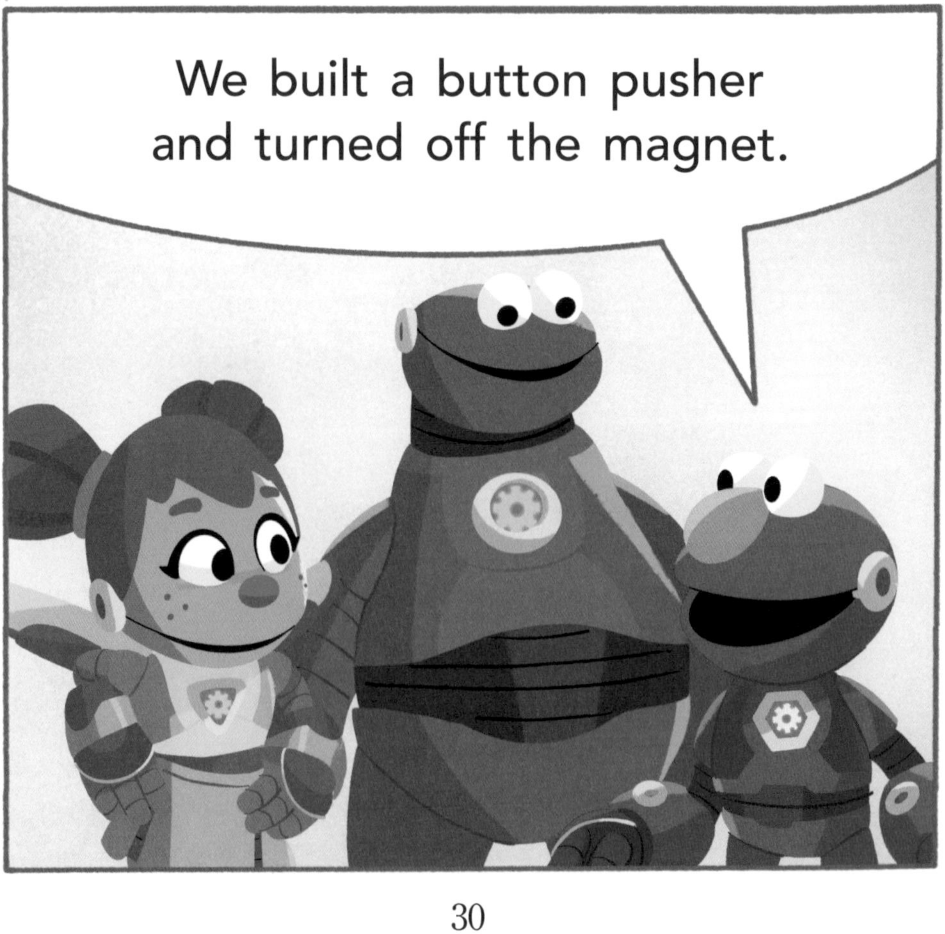
We built a button pusher
and turned off the magnet.

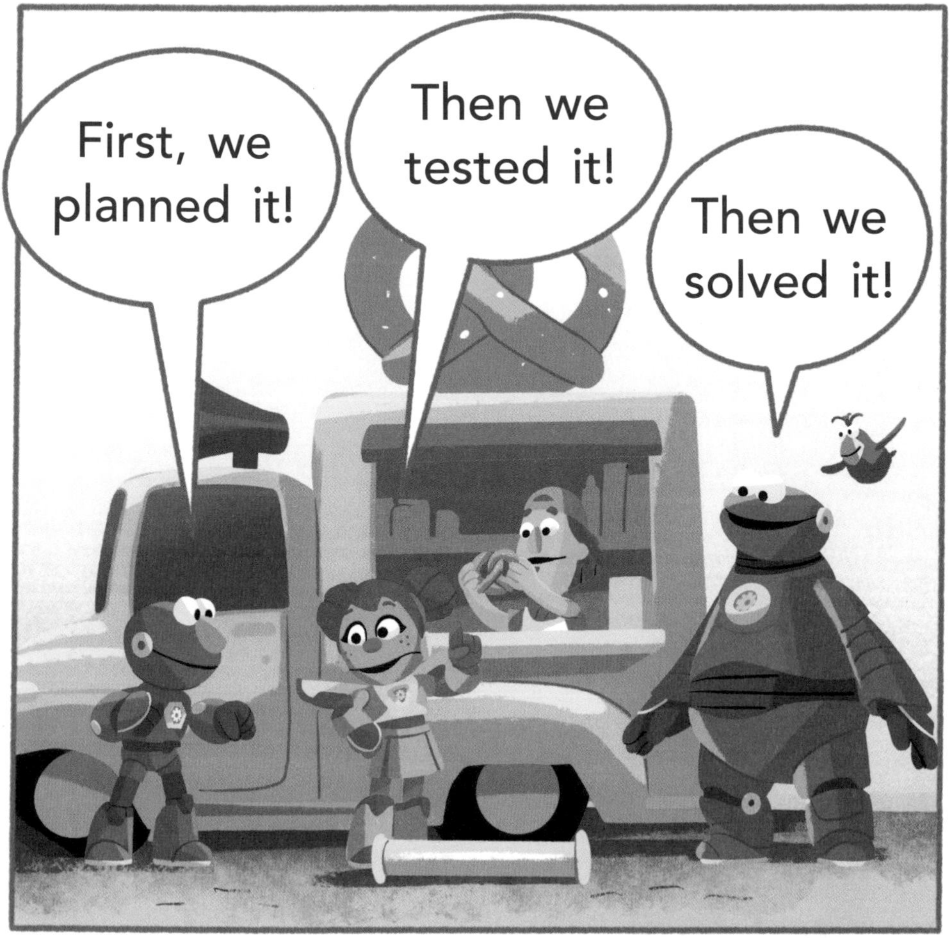
First, we planned it!
Then we tested it!
Then we solved it!

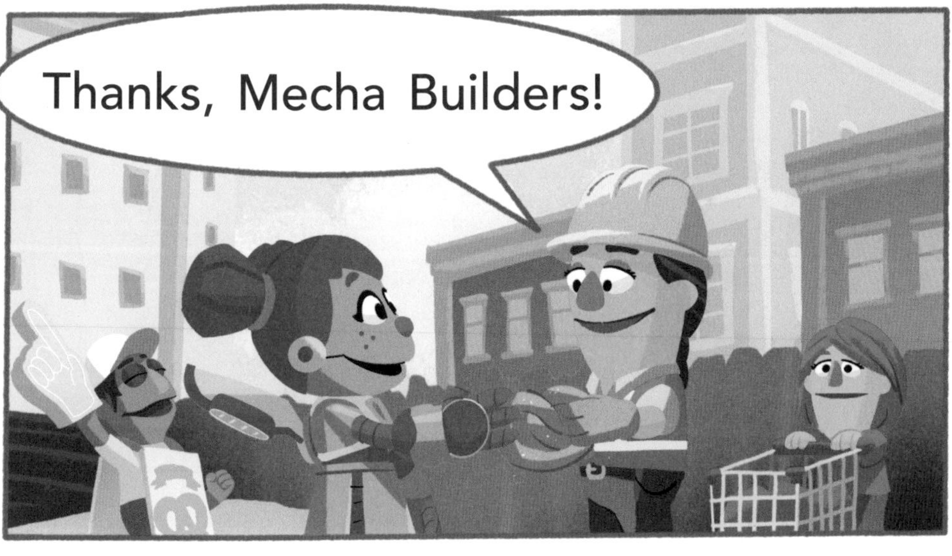
Thanks, Mecha Builders!

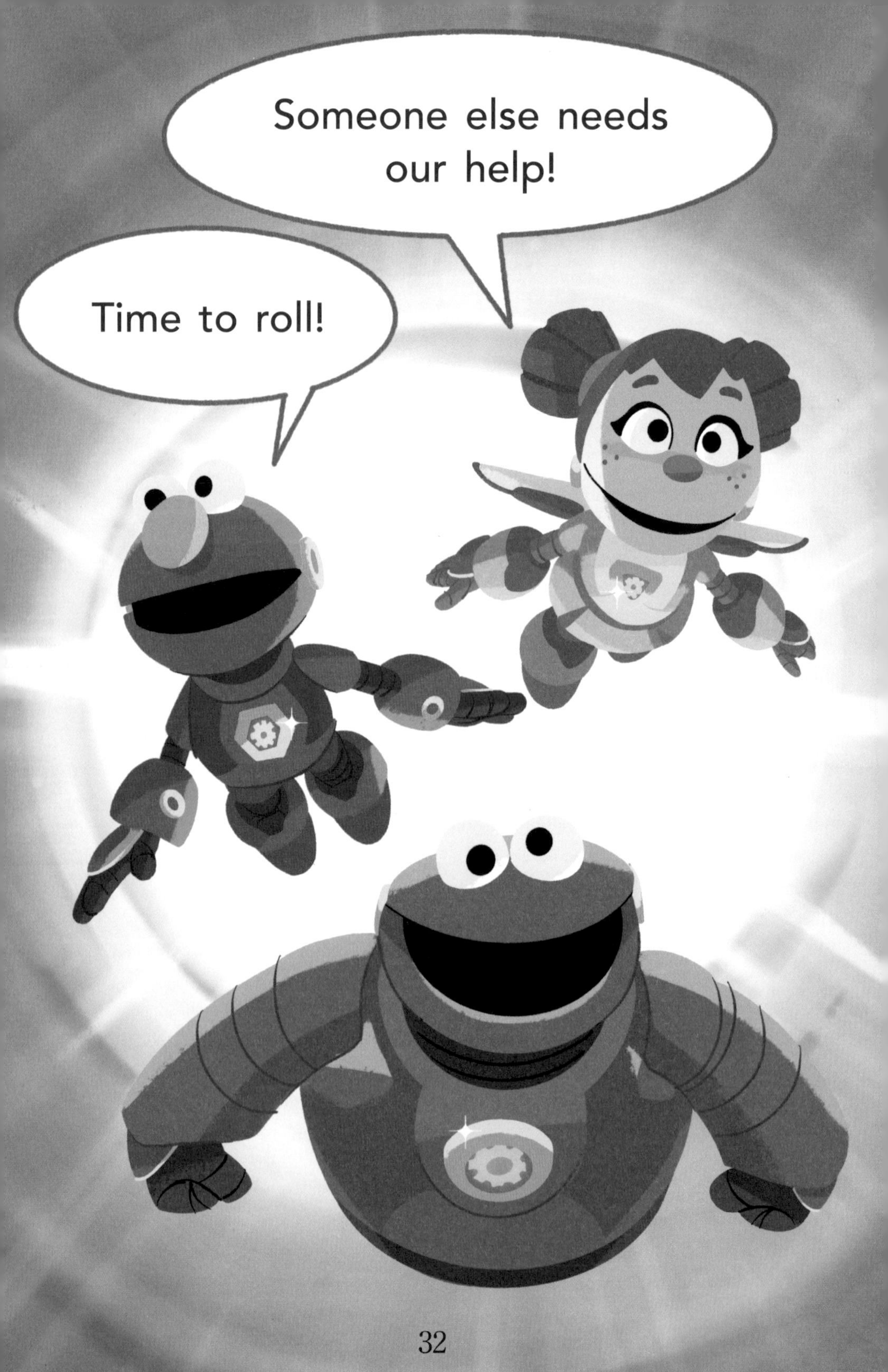
Someone else needs our help!
Time to roll!